King Penguin

Jesse Byrd

KING PENGUIN

King Penguin

Copyright © 2017 by Jesse Byrd

Library of Congress Card Catalog Number: TXu001938350

ISBN: 978-0-692-90925-6

eISBN: 978-0-692-90926-3

10 9 8 7 6 5 4 3 2 1

Printed in the United States of America

KING PENGUIN

Acknowledgments

To the mother who believed. The father who instilled. The brother who supported. The family who inspired. The friends who light the fire. And to Emaan Byrd, the love of my life.

"...hidden treasures, riches stored in secret places..."

KING PENGUIN

<u>Prologue</u>

"Where there is division, there will be strife. Splitting one group from another assures danger will follow. It begins as appreciation, sure, admiring each other's differences. But once a disagreement pushes and patience sheds its fur, those same differences become very dangerous. They become lines in the sand," Pierre's father swept his focus across their small cave.

Pierre harbored curiosity about the war for as long as he could remember. Its origins. Its persistence. Its survival. Still, he remained too timid to ask the pointed questions. This time though, since his father brought it up, he guessed now was as good of time as any. "What started our war? I mean, how did we get here?"

Pierre's father shrugs. "I was dropped into this just like you. And, I imagine, with a lot of the same questions. Some of our answers, I think, were lost in history. Others were hidden in our ancient stories and legends. But, I really believe there's not a penguin alive who is sure who struck first. Which, of course, makes everyone the victim."

Pierre scrunched his brows, finishing his first fish from the pile between them in the sand. Pierre loved when his mom brought home Mackerel from the Reserves. Mackerel was his absolute favorite. Just saying the word whisked him to a special place. But that night, not even the lure of his favorite meal could draw his attention from this particular subject.

"Then, why do it?" Pierre mumbled through his stuffed cheeks. "If we don't know why we're fighting," he swallowed it down, "why do we? Why do they? Why would anybody?"

"Because old reasons don't matter? New, fresh ones are created every day. The war's starting point might be a matter of opinion, but the loss both sides sustained and still sustain is not. This is what drives us all to sharpen our beaks. Spike our talons. Practice fighting tactics and strategies. Life! Protection. Once you've been here long enough, once you've seen this island for what it is, it covers you with a thickness. This dark cloud. A sickness, whispering to you in the night: them or us? Them or us? *Them or us?* Who will live? This voice in your head persists until *this* life is the only one you know. Until, you stop fighting it. And one day find yourself fighting to protect it. You stop questioning. Stop asking why. Stop wondering about the deeper reasons. Then, you begin to see everything as normal."

Pierre felt a warmth spread from his stomach. He frowned, looking down at the dark plot of sand he was sitting in. "This doesn't *feel* very normal."

"Death is a of life."

"Is murder?"

4

KING PENGUIN

Pierre's father crooked his neck, leaning forward. "What you don't understand, is a lot of us on this island grew up collecting food for our troops. Not troops of foreigners or strangers but mothers, fathers, cousins and friends. Seeing what we've had to see, you think we'll let this go? You think we want to? You think we could? If someone suddenly took me, your mother and your brother from you, would you let it go? When you were younger the youth weren't required to serve. Your mother and I weren't as lucky. You've never had to wrestle with these things and I get it. But, trust me, one thing I've learned here is that *everyone* deserves to be coddled. No matter where they happen to be hatched. And that feeling is worth fighting for, if and when you have to."

Pierre was still. He had other burning questions but kept quiet. His father never talked about killing. Never even alluded to it in their cave. He said, he wanted there to be peace in here. Even if this was the only place with it. After a short pause, Pierre lifted his gaze and loosened his beak.

"Have some Mackerel," his brother cut, pushing the largest piece in the pile between Pierre's webbed feet.

Craig had been sitting so quietly, Pierre nearly forgot his brother was there. Craig was a wiry, strong portrait of black and white sitting erect. He was covered in scars both healed and healing across his chest, neck, and flippers. Pierre frowned. *I get the big fish?*

5

KING PENGUIN

"Thanks," Pierre said, staring at his brother then stuffing the fish in his mouth before Craig could realize his mistake. Pierre turned back to his father, speaking with a mouthful.

"You can't…just…kill…'cause you're scared. Being scared," Pierre sat taller, "shouldn't be…the reason…we fight."

His father sighed, leaning over the pile of fish in the center. "Everyone fights for their own reasons. Some fight for love. Some for hate. Some for pride. Some for safety. *Some* for fear. And some for the future. Whatever drives each of us to the field, we all end up there. Every single one of us. Stop trying to make sense of what you're too young to understand. This is the Falklands. This is how it is here. We don't have true good and true evil. We have better and worse."

Craig shifted, "And it's worse than ever."

Pierre squinted, slyly scooting another fish from the pile in the middle to the space in front of him. "Why is it worse now?"

His father abandoned his stiff posture and slouched, peering with a glassy gaze. "Because. Built up pressure must alleviate itself."

The pale moonlight light pouring into the cave from outside suddenly disappeared. A silhouette stood in the arched entrance, lingering in the glow, before stepping in.

"Very true. And we do not want you around for the alleviation," his mom's words were soft as fresh feathers. She nodded to Pierre's father, moved across the room and sat opposite her mate.

Thoughts fired about in Pierre's mind trying to process the words. *I always ask for Mackerel, but never get it.* He thought. *Dad is actually answering questions about the war. Craig is being nice. And mom is late for dinner.* Even worse, it felt like they were speaking in code. Holding something from him. Patronizing him. Appeasing him. Pierre felt like there was a different conversation happening somewhere above his head.

His parents exchanged a gaze in the open space, then his father got up, crossed behind Craig and stood behind his partner, touching her gently at both sides. "Pierre, we sent word by albatross to my sister in Sud Afrique. You're going to stay with your aunt for a while."

"We think it's best if you stay with Patricia and Ferdinand for a while, until things cool down," his mom added.

"We'll send a word by albatross letting you know when it's safe to return."

Pierre clamped his beak so hard he felt the pressure in his temples. Fury washed over him like hot water. He erupted to his feet. "What? No! No." He shook his head. "Are you kidding me? Are you *crazy*? If it's that bad here. We'll all leave. Not *just* me!"

Pierre's mother exhaled and blinked her tired eyes. "At our age, sweetie, we'd never survive the trip."

"Plus, we're already way too many short," his father interjected. "The East needs us."

"It needs me too. As a Catcher."

"Not quite," his father rebutted. "Your brother and cousins have agreed to rotating double days on the battlefield and in the sea. They'll cover your contribution from the hunt until we get a true replacement."

Pierre's mother pushed two fish from the pile in the middle over near Pierre. "It shouldn't be difficult to make up for your catch. Now please, eat, you'll need your strength."

"Me? I'm the only one who has to go?" Pierre lifted a flipper, pointing to Craig. "I'm the *only* one!"

His mother reached for his cheek. Pierre pulled away. "You're it, sweetie. We've discussed this. Craig agrees. You're the only one young enough to start fresh yet old enough to survive the trip."

"Excuses!" Pierre yelled. "Lies and stupid excuses!" he yelled again, his face hot with anger.

Pierre's brother, sitting completely still, looked down at the two thin fish directly in front of him. "You haven't seen what we have, brother. Not fully. Not yet. You're still pure. You need to keep that and take it far away from here. I know you don't really get it and I know you don't fully understand, but that's kinda the point. We don't want you to."

"As a dad," his father stepped in. "I wanted to keep you blind. Innocent as is possible. But with you leaving, I think you deserve to know. The West has begun poisoning our food supply. Your mother had to catch these herself to make sure they were fresh before you came home. We already know of three of our Reserves which have been contaminated. The war isn't just on the field anymore."

Pierre's beak moved a tic, but nothing came out.

"They're killing our little ones!" his mother cried.

Craig hammered down, exploding bits of sand into the crisp air. He rose to his feet. "They don't deserve to live! I'll kill them all! What kind of..." Craig sniffed violently, "poison a fledgling!"

His mother shuttered. Her tears began to stream. "It's too much."

Pierre's father stepped in front of him. "This event will twist the war in darker ways than ever before. We have to get you out. So you can have a future. Look at me. A real future. Where you can take a walk with your little ones near the sea and swim with your mate in the moonlight and never have to wonder who's lurking. Never have to fear your own kind."

Pierre's father bent, searching his youngest son's face. "Don't rob us of knowing you and your future family will be safe. That they can practice belly flops and nosedives instead of beak jousts and claw thrusts."

His mother's trembling cheeks pressed two watery orbs from her eyes. "We need to know you are in a better place. Please."

"Let us have this, son." His father went and wrapped himself around his mother. "Please."

The silence hung.

Errraaaccccckkkk!

A stampede of angry squawks sounded through the night air. They all peered at the western wall of their cave, imagining what was to come.

Pierre brother grumbled looking at his parents, then his brother. "Pierre."

"Craig."

They exchanged nods and Craig exited the cave.

His father wiped his mother's face, then his own. "It's time. We've done a lot to create this distraction." His parents rushed him out to shore. "If our troops catch you trying to desert in the middle of a war, it won't be the opposite side we have to worry about. We'll all be considered traitors and face the full penalty. So, make sure you aren't being followed."

"Hopefully, this will only be for a while, sweetie. Then things will get better and we can be together again," his mother said.

As the rushed to the beach, they stopped at the edge of the water. His dad trudged a few steps into the dark, crashing waves. "Listen. Go *straight* that way," he said, pointing into the nearly pitch horizon. "Past the Georgias. Past the South Sandwiches. You should reach Bouvet in half a day's time."

"Rest there for *two* days," his mother added. "Gather your strength. Then, head north for Sud Afrique. Your aunt and uncle will be at the shore sun-fall of the third day."

His mother paused, then gasped bursting into more tears. "We love you very much. We love you very very much. Now go, while the tide is low."

"See you soon, son. We love you. Take care of your aunt and uncle."

His father hugged him longer and tighter than ever before as his mother rested her head on his side. The once far-off noises sounded closer. Pierre's father gently pried his mother away from him.

"You have to go," Pierre's father said, glancing back in the direction they came from. When he turned back to Pierre, urgency filled his eyes strong yet pleading.

Stepping backward, Pierre inched into the cool ocean, until it finally reeled him in.

KING PENGUIN

Chapter 1

Pierre stroked his flippers cautiously feeling like a tiny speck in a limitless ocean. The dark water below seemed still and empty. Yet, as a trained Catcher, Pierre knew this wasn't true. Large, slippery, teethy creatures lurked down there. Creatures which never came out during the day. Waiting. Watching. Starving.

In the pale moonlight, Pierre couldn't see far down into the dark liquid. Cool water bumped against Pierre's feathers as he swam slowly hoping not to attract any visitors. Pierre peered down into the abyss best he could checking for signs of movement.

For hours, his adrenaline eased and spiked, as he reacted to every wiggle and stir with wide eyes and stiffness. As the journey continued peacefully Pierre's edginess waned. The 'something' which always turned out to be 'nothing' led him to believe his imagination of what was down there in the dark water was more vicious than whatever truthfully could be. Pierre had pondered all sorts of ridiculous things. Sharks. Tigers. Bears. Barracudas. Tigers flinging sharks. Bears riding sharks chucking barracudas! All the terrifying stories Pierre heard of vicious animals in far-away lands mutated into a collection of visions which threatened to drive him insane if he didn't come up with a way to distract himself.

Pierre rolled onto his back, still paddling gently. Now facing the night's sky, streams of water slid down his beak and sides of his face. He was greeted by the twinkle of countless stars. Even in this scary place, seeing these 'friends' reminded him quickly that not everything is frightening, depending on where you look.

The stars off the coast of Pierre's homeland were absolutely brilliant. He spent every evening he could sitting in front of their cave watching the stars with his father. Pierre thought his dad only pretended to care about star stuff and really just sat in front of their cave to keep a lookout for danger. Still, Pierre's dad sat there, patiently debating with Pierre over his fantasies.

Pierre just left his parents and he already missed them. Thinking warmly of his mom, dad and brother, caused some tensed muscles to release. An energy spread from his chest as Pierre saw the stars doing this kind of dance-chant. A sparkling séance. Though he couldn't make sense of it, he needed this bond. He didn't speak 'star-language' but always felt connected and could never stop staring. Pierre sailed on his back thinking about the events from earlier that night. Things which would reshape his life forever, and in actuality already had. A part of him wanted to roll over and return to scanning the deep for predators and making sure he wasn't being followed by natives from his island. A reasonable concern begged him to be vigilant, but his burning questions staring up at the night's sky made this near impossible.

We're linked, Pierre believed of stars and penguins. He was certain. There was a history in their blinking code. A piece of a time past they shared with him through his recurring dreams in which the sky and ocean were switched and he swam through thin air, curving around constellations in a field of warmly glowing circles. Pierre closed his eyes, paddling along, hoping to wash ashore on this fantasy world. The ocean waves, which once roared like woken behemoths, now served as a symphony to his serenity. The wind tickled Pierre's back and he wiggled, giggling. It tickled again and he chuckled, squirming. It tickled thrice.

Pierre's eyelids sprung open. His heartbeat immediately leapt into his throat. An electricity raced through his mind arriving at a realization. *The wind couldn't tickle his back. His back was in the water.* Pierre drew a long, deep breath and turned slowly to face the ocean. Peering down into the murky abyss, to his surprise, nothing had changed. Or at least, nothing he could see. Gentle beams of light from the moon and stars still offered poor visibility. If something or *things* were down there watching him...what was it thinking of doing now? And what, if anything, could Pierre do to stop it?

Chapter 2

In Academy, every Catcher was required to complete a set of exercises as *sometimes* a penguin is the predator and *sometimes* it is the prey. The goal of these lessons was to become clever at being both. The courses, however, were painfully boring. Time moved like a slug through mud as the instructor delivered long, monotone lectures.

Pierre battled an onset of narcolepsy every period. Yet, in this moment, he yearned to recall anything of substance. Anything which might help him now. Pierre twisted his neck to get more air, then returned his focus to the water. Pieces of memory strained to come forth. The sound of a singular voice drifted like a feather in the wind and Pierre desperately chased it in his mind. Echoes. Mumbles. Laughter. Words.

"A penguin's greatest advantage," the professor said, "is sight. It's why we hunt once the sun is at its peak. Brightest time of day, you see." Pierre recalled his classroom and the raspiness of his instructor's voice.

"*Seeing* our prey is what makes us effective. And since we are much faster, the Mackerel most always becomes our meal." The professor paused for a chuckle, looked around, sighed, and continued. "Can anybody tell me *why* we are faster than fish?"

Everyone suddenly became 'distracted', finding deep interest in spaces along the cave wall. The instructor stepped forth.

"Of course," he laughed, "my question must be rhetorical. None of you have ever wondered *why* the team with the most Kings and Emperors seems to always win the team relay races?"

A hush befell the audience. As a Gentoo-King mix, Pierre remembers being as burningly curious as everyone else.

"No guesses?" The professor paused. "Okay. Guess you don't want to know the secret." The instructor threw his chin up, put his flippers at his side, and strolled toward the opening of the cave.

The class shot up in protest. Shouting, yelling and begging him to continue a lecture moments earlier they would've begged him to stop.

One Little Penguin in the back had a high-pitched voice, screeching above the rest. "Come on! Please! Tell us. We have to know. I have to know! I always come in last! I can't take it anymore!I'm tired of losing. I'm going insane!"

"Okay, o-kay, simmer. Simmer yourselves. I suppose I could proceed since you all seem to be so interested."

The instructor smacked his flippers together with great force then rubbed the tips together excitedly. "Here it comes."

The class leant so far forward Pierre thought they would topple over. The instructor gave a quick glance over both shoulders as if someone may be listening, then whispered, "When you're talking direct speed in the water, weight mostly wins. If you're little and you ever want to stand a chance against a relay team stacked full of Kings and Emperors, you need to make the course more crooked than straight."

A stupor spread across the room as one frown met another. The instructor straightened his posture, beaming as if he had just shared the meaning of life. "I want you all to remember this, because it's imperative to today's course. While the best two tools for finding food may be vision and speed, the best two tools for not being it are senses and agility. That in mind, it's time to start."

The instructor clapped twice. A clicking noise came from outside as rocks were quickly being stacked at the entrance. The cave grew darker and darker as the wall of stones rose higher and higher until the last rays were nixed and group was totally entombed. To Pierre's concern, the rocks were surprisingly well-fitting as the tiny cave became a lightless black vault.

Whispers raced with everyone talking over one another.

"Calm, calm, calm. Calm yourselves. No one here is going to hurt you. No one's going to hurt you. But, what if someone was?"

The chatter began again.

"What would be your best chance of making it out alive? Could you do something? Could you do anything?" The professor paused. "To be clear, this is not self-defense. That's silly. This is survival. And this example is designed to teach one important lesson. If, in evasion, you rely too heavily something like vision, you're a sad story waiting to be told. Imagine this room as an open ocean. An orca whale is floating so near her nose is almost brushing your beak. You're dart off! You're on the run. She has your scent. The water is dark and she's getting closer. Closer. Closer. STOP!"

The entire class yelled.

"Most make the mistake thinking looking back to see the pursuer, thinking this will help them escape. But vision is for what's in front of you. This is why your eyes have their position. When you look back, you focus more on what you're swimming from than what you're swimming to. Fear of failure will physically slow you down and steal your attention from those precious, and often fleeting, opportunities for freedom."

"I wish I had the opportunity for precious freedom right now," grumbled a voice to Pierre's left.

Footsteps advanced quickly in the sandy cave. Pierre leaned back as the sound neared. "If you want to live long enough to have waddlers of your own, Mr. Silva, stop flapping that beak and pay attention."

The instructor's hearing and sense of smell were eerily acute. The stuff of legend. Pierre heard that a student sneezed in his class once, and the instructor rattled off her diet from the last ten sunsets. Told her she needed to eat more krill.

KING PENGUIN

"I am no fool," the professor said, withdrawing from Pierre's area. "I know most of you would rather be diving off cliffs or chasing fish, but your predators are up to nine-times faster than the fastest of you and twenty-times bigger than the biggest of you. No one *ever* cares about safety until they feel unsafe but by then it is almost always too late! Correct, Mr. Silva?"

"Yes, sir," the penguin to Pierre's left responded softly.

"Brilliant! Now that it's so dark none of you couldn't see your own flipper in front of your face, I want you to close your eyes."

Pierre immediately waved a flipper in front of his face. The professor was right.

"Cease and desist, Mr. Oiseau. Put it down and bring those eyelids to-geth-er."

Creepy. Pierre squinted.

"To-geth-er," the professor repeated.

Pierre closed his eyes completely.

"Thank you. I want you to listen to my voice and sounds as I move. This will be your only guide. When you hear me step left, you step right. When you hear me on your right, move left. When I come toward you, hop back. And when I pause, *don't do anything*! A predator only stops hunting if they lost you or your scent. He or she didn't suddenly stop getting hungry, and you'll tire long before they do. What you don't want to do is help them locate you again by dragging your smell across the ocean. Give them time to clear out and go on and then swim to safety. Let's begin."

KING PENGUIN

The professor flitted about, varying speed and changing direction—sharp cuts, slow cuts, steps, stutters, stomps, pauses, blitzes, lunges, jumps, yells, whispers, claps, yips, mumbling. The students bumped and thumped into each other like a poorly choreographed dance group before catching a collective rhythm. They leaned to the four corners, swaying in unison like a school of fish.

"This is what it's about young apprentices!" The professor shouted. "*Feel her*. It's a dance. It's all a dance! Ha ha ha…"

The memory drowned back into the prison of Pierre's subconsciousness as he dropped back to the still black-blue Atlantic. He turned for another long breath, then resumed looking for a sign to free his anxiety. Something logical. A school of fish. A Blue Whale. A turtle. Turtles swim. Maybe the Mackerel gave him the gas. Or possibly_

Grrrrummmmmmmmmmmmmmmm!

The dark water rumbled as a wide cluster of circles rose, rushing past Pierre, tickling his body and face then popping at the surface. What caused the bubbles was still invisible, but three things were sadly certain: this wasn't fish. This wasn't turtles. This wasn't gas.

Chapter 3

The rumbling sound boomed through the ocean rattling Pierre's core. A dark mass glistened as it slithered up from the deeper layers. Pierre's wide eyes followed the enchanting sway as it moved closer and closer to the moonlight. Its silhouette was a husky oval with small fins and eyes which glowed a fluorescent green in the indigo water.

Swim! Pierre's mind shrieked. *No! Wait!* It rebutted. If the creature wasn't coming for him and he fled, it surely would be then. But if it were coming up for him, and he stayed, nothing could save him. The window to act was quickly evaporating. Time was running out. What was the move?

Indecision made the decision for him and Pierre instantly slouched, drifting limply about the surface like a log bobbing with the current. The beast bellowed again. He kept still as chills rippled through his frame. He was now concerned he didn't make the right choice. The creature pierced the liquid wall where the light didn't reach coming into the pale moonlight. A mass of sparkling silver fur, at least three times Pierre's length and ten times his weight. The moment had now passed to make another choice.

Pierre squinted his eyes nearly to the point of being shut as the leviathan roamed, freckles stretching its back and belly. Pierre broke cover. His eyes flashed wide, before snapping back into a squint. Those marks. Those patterns. A leopard seal.

Its long, locked teeth were bare, as the flesh which should've covered them was missing. Bubbles escaped Pierre's beak ballooning to the surface. The seal whipped to the sound, flaring its nostrils, floating in a patient stalk. Pierre's lungs went into a spasm. *Not now.* The air he released was precious and not much was left. Soon he would need a breath. His stomach quivered as he clamped his beak down firm. *No.* He thought, depriving his body. *Please*, he begged.

Pierre's vision blurred as his eyes began closing on their own. The air in his chest was noxious. If he passed out, he'd drown. If he moved and took a breath the beast would swallow him whole. No longer in control, Pierre's torso jerked as a barrage of bubbles spread into the ocean.

The seal burst toward him. Pierre leapt out of the water, gasping. Diving back down, the predator raged in pursuit. Pierre tucked his feet close to his tail, scrunching his neck between his shoulders. He popped out his flippers, paddling in quick, desperate strokes. His heart punched through his chest. The world was an aqua-blue blur. A shadow blocked the moonlight above and as

KING PENGUIN

Pierre looked up, the seal rose like smoke before darting down at Pierre. The beast's massive weight spread the water as Pierre rolled. It shot by, snatching liquid. Pierre glanced over his shoulder. The beast rose again, then sunk beneath Pierre. *Don't look back! Don't look back!*

Lunging its jagged teeth, the beast charged up. Pierre fanned to a stop. It rumbled past in a flurry, the force tumbling Pierre backward.

Pierre spun in circles until he finally got his belly down, then with a kick, he thrusted off. Crashing back into the water, the beast curved and changed trajectory. Coming in directly behind Pierre it swallowed the gap. The heat radiating from its snout was hot on Pierre's tail. Pierre cradled left. The beast bit. He cradled right. It bit again, nicking flesh. Pierre winced.

The moonlight disappeared once more as a sharp spike tinged Pierre's spine spiraling him into the abyss. In his twisting flurry, Pierre looked for a creature no longer there.

Pierre's eyes were of no more use open than closed. The ubiquitous deep made darkness seem both by his side and in the distance. He floated, unsure of what may be floating with him. What was this place stars do not touch? Pierre inched forward as something soft and slippery rolled against his foot. He snatched the foot close, darting for a spurt. As a world of sound rose to life, Pierre fathomed what each could be. Quick taps of a crab scaling rocks, the crackle and snap of an electric eel, sleepy strokes of a colossal tortoise.

What looked from above to be a vacant chasm was a vibrant society. The sounds were strange but awkwardly welcome. This bunch, creepy as they were, from all he gathered thus far, wasn't seeking to eat him. For now, that was good enough.

Taming his jitters, Pierre plotted a course north. He needed air soon, he stood no chance hiding in the monster's home and down here he was blinded in navigating to the island, possibly his best hope for safety. As Pierre ascended through the dark fluid, the lively chorus of sea life, one by one, disappeared. Left in their place was chilling silence. The whispers of a hollow pit.

Pierre swam and listened intently. Suddenly, a blinding emerald haze shone in his face as if a green veil had been drug over the sun. The glare illuminated the area. Caught in the beam, Pierre turned his face away. A clear-lit path to the upper ocean sparkled through the ghoulish glow. Pierre shot through the spectrum, shooting up out of the dark as the creature followed.

A massive chunk floated in the far reaches. Pierre couldn't make out what it was, but he didn't care. Breaking the surface again and again Pierre caught glimpses of the strange formation. The creature growled behind him, jawing, reaching. Land was in sight. The monster started to mirror Pierre, hopping in and out of the water, drawing near.

Splish. Splash. Splish. Splash. Splish. Splash.

Pierre pulling away, the beast cut deep, down to the center of the Earth swimming in a fury. Down! Down! Down! Down! Down!

Up! Up! Up! Up! In glitches, it bolted from the trenches as a hard pop pushed Pierre into orbit. Bursting through the surface, the seal hauled its ten-foot frame into the cold night air. Its jaw flung open and half of Pierre's body fell into its mouth. Slimy wet moisture, dripping and lukewarm rubbed against Pierre's back. Pierre shut his eyes tucking his lower half as teeth rattled shut behind him.

Flailing toward the Atlantic, the beast crashed like a Humpback rippling massive waves. Pierre followed, skipping like a rock across the top of the ocean. Flipping into different positions each time he hit the surface. Six lashing skips, and the water turned solid. Pierre slid across a smooth surface slamming into a vertical sheet of ice.

Every wisp of wind was kicked from his lungs. An inhale sent knifing pains to his chest and ribs. Twisted in a sprawl, Pierre lay limp on white tundra.

Dawn broke, as a new sun reflected off the ice changing everything an orange-cream color. Figures bounced on the horizon. Pierre warred for consciousness. Drooping his head against the hard surface, Pierre heaved an exhale.

Chapter 4

Twitching awake, Pierre's body was stretched across a firm surface. It was cold. His breaths were small, shallow and constricted. A binding tightness around his chest and stomach made taking air difficult as thick bands of seaweed were wrapped tight from under his flipper to the mid of his stomach. Pierre tilted his head and found a makeshift bed of kelp in the corner sunken with a heavy dent. Mixed aromas of supper and stench floated about. Scanning the domed surroundings, Pierre tried to find the source of the smells, hoping one smell had nothing to do with the other.

"G'morning, sunshine," something spoke. "It's about flippin' time you woke up. I was getting ready to roll you up and put you back where I found you."

Pierre couldn't find the speaker.

"Hey!" It griped again. "What do you want me to rub 'em for ya? Get ya webbies out of my face!"

KING PENGUIN

There was a slap at his left foot. Sassy yellow eyes glared up at him between his webbed feet. The eyes belonged to a penguin half Pierre's height and twice his weight.

Pierre frowned.

"Who did I get here and when am I?" he asked, mustering his strength.

"Beg your pardon?" The stranger said.

Pierre sat up, grimacing. Pain shot like flashes of lightning through his frame. He straightened his posture from a slouch. "Mmph. You see what I said, give me some questions or I'm laying right down and I'm leaving!"

"Oof! Goodness." The strange portly penguin hobbled toward Pierre. Pierre slid himself back on the ice. The stranger stopped and stared as if making a very serious decision. Then, in a swift motion, the penguin bent, nipping at something below Pierre's line of sight. All Pierre could see was the top of his head twitching and moving as sounds of a clicking beak snapped through dome.

"Eat," he commanded.

The stranger lobbed a sumo-sized chunk of meat through the air. It sailed over the top of Pierre's head.

"Eat the fish." Another chunk of meat whisked past his left eye. Another came, which smacked his forehead and fell in front of him before slipping off the side of the icy slab.

"Eat the fish." he repeated in a flat, even tone.

"Ow!" Pierre exclaimed as another bit of meaty ammunition popped him in the right shoulder.

Pierre realized he would eventually be beat senseless if he didn't do as he was told. Pierre twisted his neck and caught the next chunk as it zipped past his right ear. The thick, soft slice was gobbled and slid down his throat as Pierre tilted his beak to the sky. Another piece immediately followed. It was so large it filled every empty space in Pierre's mouth. Both of his cheeks swelled like a blowfish.

"Better?" asked the mysterious host.

Pierre nodded. "Is...is that chub?"

The host paused, frowning. He looked at Pierre, then at his gut, then back at Pierre. "I may have put on a pound or two since I came out of the egg, but I'd *hardly* call it chub."

"The fish. Is it Chub?"

"Oh, yea. Fresh harvest of the Galapagos Islands!"

"*The Galapagos*! Is that where I am?"

"With this weather? You must be a coo-coo bird."

"Then how did you get the fish?"

"I know a bird who knows a bird. Mind your business."

"Oh."

"But you're definitely here, not there."

"Where's here?"

"Nowhere most of the time. Somewhere some of the time."

"Which is it now?"

"Most of the time," he smiles. "How I like it."

Pierre's felt his head throbbing. Each pump of his heart pulsating painfully in his brain. Yet, there were serious and sensitive questions which *needed* answering. "How did I get here?"

"You mean in general?"

"Yes."

"You mean you don't know?"

"No."

"No clue at all?"

"No."

"*Really?*"

"No!" Yelling hurt Pierre's chest.

"I thought you would've put one and one together by now. Let me see if I can explain: when two penguins love each other very, very much and they want to express that deep, profound, burning, passionate commitment. When there's no one else they'd rather talk to. When ordinary stuff, especially ordinary stuff, seems a million times more special. And it's that season, that *special* season when everybody's all hot and riled up _"

"Noooooo! Stop it. Not how did I come into this world, how did I get into this place, this cave?"

The miniature penguin exhaled. His entire body seemed to deflate. "That's easy. I carried you."

"*You*...carried...*me*?"

"Yup." The penguin looked up as if to focus on a point in the ceiling. "Threw you over my shoulder. Trekked the width of this great island fending off predator's southpaw and battling the worst of the elements! Beak frozen shut. Snow up to my hip. And wind! Wind so strong a lesser bird would've been blown to sea." The host solemnly dropped his focus as if paying respects to the dead before snapping back to his regular tone. "And it's not a cave. It's a dome."

Pierre examined the short penguin's physique. Looking up, down and around for anything he may have missed "But you *carried* me?"

"Yeah. What you don't think I could? It's not all blubber, young flipper there's some muscle under here too," he said, poking his body, looking for proof. "Somewhere."

Pierre squinted slowly tilting his head

"Okay! You're no fun. I dragged you. Nipped you on the wing and hopped backward. Stopped a couple times, weather was pretty good, and I could see you pretty clear from the front entrance -- but who cares! What matters is you're in here and not out there."

Pierre still wasn't very sure where *here* is. Pierre desired to ask more questions in an attempt to decipher the stranger's motives, but he settled on the ideal that if harm were intended from this penguin it could have already been done.

Pierre felt muscles, which he didn't know were tense, unclench. The alluring draws of his appetite suddenly returned and clawed at his mind until he could concentrate on little else for more than a few seconds. *How long has it been since he's eaten?* His stomach was turning on itself.

"Fish?" Pierre asked, leaning toward the pile.

"Sure. Have as much as you like. I get tons of that stuff."

Pierre eased from the slab, wincing, then teetered, staggered, and caught his balance. He crept tenderly to the supply of fish which he now saw was hidden in a hole in the floor near the foot of where he had been laying. Now that they were both up and standing, the small penguin was actually a little below half of Pierre's height -- as the crown of the penguin's head reached Pierre's mid-stomach.

"I've never been this hungry." Pierre said plunging his beak into the hole filled with fish.

"And this fish, augh, it's so good!" He closed his eyes. Then lifted one half-open. "You sure this is Chub? This can't just be Chub. I've had Chub and–" Pierre went in for another, cutting his own sentence short.

"It's Chub, trust me. Anything would taste good after three days."

"Three days!" Pierre nearly choked, clearing his throat. "I was out for three days!"

"Give or take, yeah, who's counting?"

"I'm supposed to be at Sud Afrique by sun-fall today!"

KING PENGUIN

"Well, there's no need to get fluffy. Sud Afrique is just a waddle away from old Bouvet. I'll show you where to jump in the water and point you in the right direction. Grab a few more of those fish you nearly insulted me earlier with and follow me." The short penguin pivoted one hundred and eighty degrees and wobbled out the doorway.

This is Bouvet. Pierre sighed. *There's still time to meet aunt and uncle.* Pierre's mind felt clearer and the pains in his chest, back, and ribs were less intense. Eating as much as he could, Pierre then ducked under the small exit and hustled to catch pace.

As Pierre stepped outside, shades of pale blue reflected from the glacial mountains and decorated the skyline. The expanse was covered in both stretches of smooth glistening ice and soft powdery snow. The blankness of the tundra brought with it a strange calm. Everything stoic and still. The small penguin bustled along gingerly tossing his head from left to right. His quick but short strides allowed Pierre to keep pace without much effort. As they walked across the open space Pierre thought the penguin might say something. A few days ago, this mysterious penguin had saved his life, nursed him to health, offered his home, his rations, and what Pierre thinks could possibly be his bed -- surely, he must have some questions himself. *At least you think he'd ask my name.*

"What's your name?" the stranger asked.

Oh.

"Pierre Oiseau"

KING PENGUIN

"That French?"

"I dunno."

"You French?"

"No, I'm from East Falkland of the Falkland Islands. You?"

"Paul Jaunty. I'm home anywhere everyone is not."

"I take it you don't like penguins very much."

Paul snorted a chuckle, "Ya think?"

"Can I ask why?"

"Couldn't hurt."

"Why?"

"Don't worry about it. The real question is how a bird your age ends up completely passed out in the middle of *my* nowhere," Paul said, motioning a grand gesture to the icy desert. "What's your story?"

Pierre opened his beak, closed it shut, then opened it again. "There's a war back home between the two islands. It's always been that way. Things weren't always as bad as they are now, but they were never good. Time came when bad quickly turned *too bad* and my parents sent me to live with family in Sud Afrique. On my way here, I was attacked by a leopard seal, swam like krill and ended up here."

Paul tilted his neck. "I don't believe it."

"Me either. Sent off alone through a dangerous ocean to a place I've never been, to stay with family I don't know or remember. To top it off, I don't know when I'll be able to go back, or even if," Pierre huffed.

Paul stared up at Pierre. "I don't believe *you* wondered why I don't like penguins. Look at this crummy life of yours. Sent away from a family it sounds like you *actually* wanted to be with to live with what might as well be strangers, because of this fight that had nothin' to do with you."

Pierre's thoughts ran to his parents.

"Trust me," Paul continued, "one penguin, fine. Two, *mmmmaybe*, but once those braying blubber-butt birds get into a waddle they quickly find a way to destroy *something* and it's only a matter of time before they find ways to destroy *everything*."

Paul grumbled to himself some more as Pierre looked across the landscape. "If you hate penguins so much, why'd you carry me back to your cave?"

"*Dragged.* And *dome.*"

"And get me the fish?"

"I had the fish."

"And take care of me?"

"Hey! Quit it! Don't get so high on yourself, this was a favor."

"How can I return it?" Pierre asked

"Not for you, Pierre. For someone else. I was told once, and only once, my life is the sum of my decisions. I *know* I'm the only penguin on this island...or at least I'd sure better be. That means I *know* if I walk away you die. That's it! Fin. You go directly up to the Celestial Nest.

Life has shown me I'm tough even if when I didn't want to be, but I can't live with that. If you *know* you can help, and someone really needs it, how is that a choice?"

Pierre slowed, allowing his host lead the way without shuffling. Pierre swept his gaze across the snowy deserted wasteland which felt equally captivating and desolate. Aside from the whistle of the wind and their tapping talons on ice the island was hush. Beautiful as this place it felt more than empty. It felt unalive. A complete opposite of the dark ocean which only 'played dead' this place really seemed dead. Like something stuck in time with a stolen life force. This nothingness Pierre sensed from the island was an eerie feeling he had yet to experience, and one he never really wished to again.

"You ever get lonely?"

"I couldn't spell the word. Being alone is a great thing. You get to do what you want, when you want, where you want! And after the last stain of formality from society washes clean, and you stop looking over your shoulder and you absolutely, positively know you're never ever ever being watched you get to meet someone. You. The real you. *The disgusting you.* I'll give an example, I like to fart in the ocean." Paul shrugged. "Go figure. Never knew. I enjoy the warmth and the bubbles tickle my body."

A sour image crossed Pierre's mind. He frowned.

KING PENGUIN

Paul nobly lifted his chin. "Ah. The look of a bird who doesn't know what he's missing. What a pity. Point is, it makes me happy. When I lived in a colony I was way too afraid. Too afraid of what birds might say and worse what they might not say yet think. Would they like me? Would they respect me? Would they want to be seen with me? Would I find a mate being *that* way? I may be a little funny. I'll admit that. I may not have any friends. I will admit that too, but Paul Solomon Jaunty knows *and* is passionately in love with Paul Solomon Jaunty."

Paul's brisk steps came to a halt. "Here we are." He bowed. "Swim that way." Paul pointed across the water with his wing. You'll be there in no time." Paul turned and walked away.

Pierre slid to the edge of the ice peering into the liquid. He pushed clumps of snow into the water with his foot then watched them disappear

"It's water," Paul said bending slowly back into the frame. "You swim in it."

Pierre exhaled, taking a long blink. "After what happened to me--"

"You're going to live life not swimming because of one stupid seal?"

Pierre raised his eyebrows, thinking.

"C'mon. It was one tough swim. You can't let that hold you forever. You have somewhere to be, the water is how you get there. Boom. Go."

KING PENGUIN

Gazing down at the sea, Pierre touched the seaweed around his stomach and took two steps back.

"Okay, okay. I get it. You still got the oooga ba-boogas. How about this, I'll swim with you, watch your back. You'll be safe. No one knows these waters better than me. I'll make sure you don't get eaten by something hungry and vicious with sharp scary teeth."

"Thanks," Pierre whispered.

"Don't thank me. I want my sleeping spot back. *You* gotsta go." Paul looked to the sky, "Hmm. I should be home before dark."

The sinking sun reeled its beams of light back into the source as the pale blue sky wore streaks of lavender and amber. Time was fading. If Pierre failed to reach South Africa by dusk, he'd be stuck in the dark ocean. Paul Jaunty or not, Pierre wasn't mentally equipped to spend another night in his nightmare.

Pierre's mind raced through scenarios. If he was late, his aunt and uncle might return to report the news, leaving Pierre alone on a dark night without any guide in a strange land. This is assuming he even picked the right shore. Or he could get separated from Paul and lose his way. Then end up swimming endlessly (or as long as he could stay alive). Or docking somewhere entirely wrong and being stranded, wandering from beach to beach until he's old in age. Or reaching an island which seems safe but is really more dangerous than the open sea. Again, his imaginings ran away with him.

Pierre wished he had more days to recover. From everything. Bending to ease himself into the water, he made a faint ripple and slowly ebbed from the icy shelf.

Suddenly, he heard intense gasping and grunting. He looked around, then up to glimpse Paul charging toward the ocean. Pierre's eyes grew large as sand dollars.

SMMAACKCK!

The rattling sound pierced the cold, quiet air as Paul Jaunty belly-flopped into the South Atlantic. Pierre froze. He felt anything with sharp teeth was surely splitting the sea right now to their location. Pierre turned for land but Paul's stiff, sharp beak somehow already stuck in his back.

"Thataway. You watch the front, I'll cover the rear. We'll go above water. I wouldn't recommend you diving too deep for a day or two. That seaweed wrapped around your ribcage is good for healing but not so good for the breathing. Better birds than you have drowned still recovering not knowing the limits of their wind. Didn't go through the inconvenience of becoming a hero for nothing."

Cool liquid sloshed and slapped against Pierre's body as they pushed further into the Atlantic. The passage thus far was slow and Paul wasn't shy in sharing his thoughts on the pace.

"Are you expecting, Pierre? Are you with egg? I know a Rockhopper named 'One-Fin Willy.' Swim circles around you."

Paul slung insults as Pierre did his best to ignore.

KING PENGUIN

"You've got two speeds, kid. Slow and reverse," Paul continued.

After a while, the comments chimed as no more than white noise. Pierre looked straight ahead and eventually, somehow managed to tune him out.

When at last shore was in sight Pierre spun to thank Paul for all he had done. But he only found a vast, empty sea. Pierre remembered Paul griping about an aching throat a number of strokes back. Pierre wasn't sure exactly when Paul disappeared. Or how long he had been swimming alone. Perhaps, Paul Jaunty never intended to take him the whole way. But it didn't matter. A duet of black and white penguins stood waving from the sand up ahead.

Chapter 5

"*Pee-Pee!* Is that you?" two birds asked in unison.

Pierre forced a smile. No one called him that in a long time and he wished it would've stayed that way.

"That *is* you! You're taller. But you've still got the same little beak," his Aunt Patricia exclaimed and batted him on the muzzle. Pierre saw his Aunt Patricia was a healthy Adelie with strong black and white lines which didn't at all touch or mix with splashes of yellow from her King penguin heritage. "We told everyone you were coming! We were getting worried you might not make it."

"*She* was getting worried," said a thin Magellanic with a long neck standing beside his aunt Pierre presumed this to be Uncle Ferdinand. The black and white patterns of his feathers reminded Pierre of a miniature orca whale. "I knew a strong swimmer, such as yourself, could handle whatever came along." Uncle Ferdinand paused to examine Pierre's attire. "Got a hot date?" he pointed, laughing at the seaweed around Pierre's chest and stomach.

"I had a run in with a leopard seal on the way. This is supposed to help me heal."

"It's healing kelp! Oh my, are you alright?" his aunt said, shrieking sharply.

Ferdinand frowned, leaned over and whispered to Pierre, "She's not usually like this." Then, Uncle Ferdinand stood tall, "Of course he's all right! Your father's stock you are. Did you give 'em the old two to the body, one to the jaw routine?" Ferdinand asked, ducking and fighting an invisible foe on the shore.

"I swam like krill. Barely escaped with my life."

"Oh," Ferdinand said as his shoulders sank. "I guess that's okay too."

Patricia turned and chopped Ferdinand in the stomach folding him in half.

"There she is," Ferdinand wheezed.

Patricia lurched over Ferdinand's bent body, "It's more than okay. Your nephew is safe." Carefully embracing Pierre at both sides, she reminded him of the pure insanity his uncle has always been plagued with. "Some penguins love the idea of a fight," she said loud enough for Ferdinand to hear, "but they wouldn't have a clue what to do if they actually had to."

Ferdinand emerged from the faded brown sand catching his breath. "Patricia, I just ate. Have you no shame?" Ferdinand caught up and walked on the opposite side of Pierre. "Sometimes that one still thinks she's back home in the Falklands," he mumbled.

As they set out toward the colony, the new land looked a lot more like home. Sand and gravel in lieu of ice and snow. Shades of green, grey, and brown across the land versus blue and white. Their path veered and they stopped at a split in the road.

"This trail leads to the forest," Ferdinand said, noticeably more serious. "We share this land with some dangerous things. Don't ever go there. Only our Scavengers know the secret and safe trails."

Pierre lingered as the myrtle and olive branches stretched from the winding path into the forest. Even with the aid of the fading light, after a mere ten to twelve steps in that direction there appeared to be a solid wall of black. Behind which screeches, caws, hoos, barks, and buzzings were sleepily coming to life. Pierre looked up to the tall crooked, leafy trees which curved over the domain. Patricia ushered them left.

Final moments of warmth emanated from the setting sun as night took center stage. A path of small, carefully laid white stones, cracked into different shapes met the sandy trail as they approached the pass. Walking between two gigantic beige mountains the three of them eased down a small slope into a society settling for slumber. Starlight imparted the beach with a luminous glow. The moon pressed a wide wavering streak, sparkling and majestic, on the dark ocean.

A tiny penguin jumbled into view gasping and giggling as it crossed the sand being chased by a larger penguin. A trip, a fall, and the race was over.

KING PENGUIN

"I said it's bedtime," the larger penguin decreed, brushing the sand from the little one's body. Patting him on the beak, she nudged the smaller penguin into a silverish dome. Scores of like structures dotted the moonlit beach. Each filled with the rustlings of a day's end.

"Welcome to Caterwaul," Pierre's uncle said. "The finest colony by the sea." Ferdinand held his wings out wide with his back to the rolling waves. "Of course, the full tour will have to wait till in the morn."

Pierre's aunt asked if he was hungry and Pierre respectfully declined. He was exhausted. What Pierre wanted most was rest. He followed Ferdinand and Patricia to the dome they called home. A stand-alone cave in the sand. In it was little more than two sleeping spaces made up of big green leaves and soft sand pushed into a lump. Ferdinand and Patricia showed Pierre to his place in the sand and bid him goodnight.

His aunt pushed the cool grains closer to his body and pulled an enormous, plush green leaf up to Pierre's chest with her beak. "First thing tomorrow, we'll send Tiberius to tell your parents you've made it safely. But for now, rest." She pressed her forehead firmly against his, held it there for a moment, then turned and left.

Sleep for Pierre came like a skillful, swift bandit stealing him into the night.

Chapter 6

As Patricia paced to her side of the dome she was brimming. Her nephew's arrival brought with it an unspeakable joy. Patricia always admired her brother for staying, and even more so for the reasons he did. The choice was honorable and brave but Pierre being here now meant one less penguin flourishing in a morbid hole of death and murder. Caterwaul was a better home. A safer home. A place to have a future. And Patricia pledged to keep that true from the day she discovered the colony.

Through her endless voyage escaping the Falklands and all it represented, Patricia was never fully sure anything existed across the sea. From the coast of their home, the ocean looked like it dropped off into nothingness. Or maybe beyond a certain point somehow you would end up in the sky around where the sky and ocean touched.

Patricia escaped the East Falklands in search of a white island. Not because it was better, but because it was the only other place she'd ever heard of. The tale of the white island was told to her again and again in a bedtime legend, "Somewhere where the water stops. The ground is cold and hard as rock. A place most don't dare to go. A place of quiet, still, and snow." The story told of an island where everything was white, still, and no one could be seen for stretches on the clearest afternoons. She wasn't sure it existed. Maybe the story was a fake. Or a metaphor for the Celestial Nest. Maybe it was empty hope. Maybe so, but she had to try.

When she set out, the massive, crushing waves seemed to mock her guile, pushing hard against her strong strokes as thrashing wind stole her momentum, making her swim double. By the time the storm calmed, the only thing she knew was it wasn't dark anymore. Her flippers were still moving but her eyes were closed. Something soft swept up under her.

She blinked and slowly pulled herself to a stance. The sun was glaring. The sand was twinkling, and the water danced with sparkles. This wasn't the island she sought. Exhaustion closed in on her quickly, inducing a shocked delirium. She couldn't trust her eyes. *Was this real? Did I die?*

Three strangers approached. Patricia staggered back and even in her dizzied state she managed to drop them in five moves: Stomach. Throat. Head. Neck. Ribs. Then, she collapsed.

When she woke, there were no less than twenty penguins around her. She labored again to a stance, ready to be engaged for a second time. The crowd kept a distance. She spun every two seconds, checking her six, until a medium sized Chinstrap stepped forward. "What's your name?" he said in a commanding tone.

Patricia kept her stance, monitoring her peripheral. They had good numbers and not all of them were small.

"Patricia," she responded, her voice cracking.

"Well, *Pat-ricia*, I'm the Sachem. I'd like to know why you assaulted our Medics."

"I thought they were attacking me."

"*Attacking* you? Why in Blue Cod would they *attack* you?"

She frowned. "Because I'm not from around here."

"That sounds silly. You sound silly. We don't *attack* penguins here. This is a society. One crèche. One circle. You understand?"

Patricia nodded slightly.

"Good. Now walk with me over to the Reserve. We have something to discuss."

Patricia didn't want to go anywhere with him. Especially alone. Yet, she knew she was in no condition to flee back to the ocean and lacked the strength to fight twenty or more birds. She followed the Sachem trailing a few paces back until they reached a giant tan and grey slab. The construct was made up of several pebbles and stones with varying patterns which swirled upon each rock. If Patricia ran thirty strides along the length of this thing, she wouldn't be to the other end.

The Sachem stopped and pointed at the supply. "Eat," he commanded.

46

KING PENGUIN

Did she have a choice?

"Eat," he said, standing straight.

Was it poisoned? Was it free?

Patricia stepped to the raised slab. The rim met her midsection. She leaned over, picked a tiny piece of brown flounder, and swallowed it with an up-thrust of the neck. The Sachem grumbled, etching closer.

"More," he said, standing over her right shoulder. Glaring into the massive mound of fish.

She had another. He nodded. She kept going. Four! Six! Seven! Nine! Twelve! She looked back at the aggressive white and black faces staring at her. Though Patricia was taller than most of the penguins, she didn't feel in control.

"That's enough," he finally said.

Patricia stepped away feeling slightly more alert. "Are you the leader?" she asked.

"The leader?"

She nodded.

"No such thing," he said. "I'm in charge of food, and they respect me for it, but I don't pretend to tell them what they can and can't do."

She swallowed. "How do you all stay safe?"

"From what? You're the most dangerous thing we've seen. Everything that might hurt us is out in that ocean." He pointed to the horizon.

KING PENGUIN

Patricia looked across the landscape of the shore. Two caves at each end. One cave extended like a tunnel almost down to the shore and another, smaller cave that sat back about fifty steps from the water. Massive twin mountains met in the middle and completely walled the southern half. This was an oasis. There were tiny lumped hills, which didn't really look like hills, in various places with tiny openings.

"What are those?" Patricia asked, unsure if the question was beyond her right to know.

"Those are the domes. We sleep in them. Think of it as a small personal cave on the sand. One of our best minds built those a while back, but since then has left."

She wanted to explore these new creations, but thought better of poking her head in on unsuspecting families after beating up locals.

"Patricia," the Sachem said coarsely, strangely enunciating the first three letters. "It is *Pat*-ricia, correct?" He repeated.

"Yes."

"Where exactly were you headed when you landed here? Where did you mean to be?"

"I'm not sure." That wasn't entirely true, but she couldn't entirely perceive his motives.

He ran his gaze up her tall stature.

"Where did you come from?"

"Somewhere I didn't want to be. Somewhere penguins attack penguins without thinking."

"Humm. Well, if you don't know where you're going, and don't want to be where you came from, you can stay here."

Something of an electric shock snapped through her body.

"There's more than enough food, and room, and stuff. Just, dagnabbit, no more beatings!"

Patricia stood completely still.

"You can stay with our friendliest resident. He stays alone. Name's Ferdinand, he's stays over there." The Sachem pointed to a row of domes not bothering to specify which. "If you've had enough fish," he nodded encouragingly.

She nodded in return.

"Then, you can retire. You look exhausted. We'll reconvene in the morning, and give you the tour. For now, rest." The Sachem walked down the shore so close to the flow that the waves hit him every eight steps.

"Hold it!" She yelled, louder than intended. Citizens within an earshot stopped what they were doing and spun around. "Sorry," she said.

They went back to their work.

"Why're you doing this?" She caught up to the Sachem.

He shook his head and grinned. "Because that's how we are. Stay if you want or, don't."

Patricia's heart thumped. She cleared her throat. Walking to the domes to search for her host, she suddenly broke into a tired sob.

Recalling the series of events, the locals must've thought her mad. Fighting, yelling, eating, crying. In the following days, Patricia convinced the Sachem that the outside world was dangerous and Caterwaul should set up a system of defense. She wanted this place to remain pure as she found it. She taught a small force of volunteers how to guard the borders and patrol the landscape. As the group explored the far reaches of the Cape, citizens understood more and more the threats which lie dormant in the forest and her number of pupils grew. Patricia took ownership over of the budding force and the little ones started calling her "Safety." She didn't like taking the credit. She was a part of a team. Yet, the idea of taking her dangerous past and using it for something good was heartwarming.

Now, she had the chance to share this place with her youngest nephew. But for him to remain here for long, there was something she must do.

Chapter 7

For Pierre, morning arrived a lot sooner than he'd hoped. On the very heels of dawn, Ferdinand woke Pierre stammering and making noise about something Pierre desperately needed. Pierre trailed Ferdinand out of the dome. His aunt stood in the daybreak, whispering a strange dialect in the ear of a giant bird.

"Is *that* your albatross?" Pierre inquired.

"Tiberius Flock, in the feather," his uncle smiled.

"I can't make out what she's saying."

"Be surprised if you could. Few penguins can speak the old language. Which is why we started teaching a more common lingo some time ago. Your father will understand the message, but to most everyone else, it's just gibberish."

"Is that why we're up so early?" Pierre straightened from a hunch. "So I can learn the old language?"

"No. You need a job."

"A job?"

"Precisely. This colony doesn't have many rules, Pierre, but one the citizens enforce without mercy is the *CC* or Contribution Clause. Now come, or we'll miss the whole thing."

Rushing across the shore, the two brake at a crowd standing in parallel bunches with an aisle running through the middle. Nudging through the assortment of Adelies, Chinstraps, Magellanic, Humboldt, Macaroni, and Snares, Pierre and his uncle stumbled to the forefront. Ferdinand propped a flipper and tapped Pierre. Pierre stepped back from the trail.

"What's happening?" Pierre asked

"Shh," his uncle uttered along with a stranger to his right.

Pierre followed the collective focus down a gaping beige aisle.

"No. No! Please!"

Pierre heard, but could not see.

"I swear. It was only for a little while. Only for a little while. I didn't *mean* anything by it!" Cried someone shoved down the aisle.

The sun's glare obstructing full view, Pierre could only recognize it as a male, slightly taller than most.

Two Emperors pushed the body without concern. Passing Pierre's line of view, the captive contorted and broke loose, crawling to an Adelie across the aisle, clinging to her side.

"Caroline, please!" he begged, his back to Pierre. "I was tired. I just needed a break, I was going to get right back. Right back! I was going to get back."

The female stared across the way. "I'm sorry. It's cost too much. There's no excuse." She shook him from her lower half as the Emperors each stuck a flipper under his.

The victim kicked and huffed. He wriggled and wrung and jerked before being head butted in the temple. Pierre watched the action from behind.

Heads swiveled in turn as the event passed their line of sight. At the end of the path, the three arrived at that narrow space between the two mountains Pierre entered the previous night. Ferdinand signaled for them to move closer. Squeezing into position, a large bird hovered high above the captive.

The Emperors stopped and circled around to face the crowd, holding the penguin.

"Citizens of Caterwaul. You have condemned this resident to permanent Banishment," said the one to the right.

"You've deemed him unfit for the pleasures of our society," followed the one on the left.

"If any penguin wishes to plead on his behalf, now will be your only forum."

"After which, this decision is permanent."

"Thus, any allies to his cause step forward and make your claim now."

Murmurs swelled. In hushed tones the citizens held court. Pierre did his best to follow as conversation shot around him. Once discussions ceased and silence sustained, words again came from the Emperors on the mount.

"The decision is absolute then."

The Emperors turned to the guilty party. Muscles tightened in Pierre's stomach.

"Solus Ravillac, you have been accused and convicted by your peers," said the one to the right.

"To be a cancer and leech upon this community," followed his massive partner to the left.

"You will be branded a pariah and placed amongst those no longer welcome in this place."

"Return, under any circumstances, and you will be killed immediately."

"Do you have any parting remarks?"

The captive allowed his full weight to hang on his oppressors. Head drooped and body hung low, his beak parted with no sound before standing erect.

"There will be a day. A day in which none of you are safe. It will come while you work and play and sleep and on the face of *this* day there will know no mercy. The tall and the small, penguins with strength and penguins without will be equally helpless. If you only knew what was on the horizon you would keep me and consider me a truth seer, because it has done so much killing and it is knocking upon Caterwaul. Hunting and building is useless. Yet, when the truth of these words comes crawling to your shore, it will be too late. But, merely spare me and I will share my findings and do the same. Citizens of Caterwaul, this isn't my last chance, it's yours."

Chatter rounded the crowd as everything from frowns to smiles were in plain view. Shade between the mountains hid the prisoner's upper half, but Pierre noticed something glinting as he spoke.

The Emperors extracted something with their beak from small holes in the rocks. Carving the victim in what looked like the flippers, Solus howled and twitched. Replacing their tools, the Emperor cawed to the bird floating in the sky. An echo returned and the captive vanished behind the hill.

Chapter 8

"What. Just. Happened?" Pierre asked, confused.

Ferdinand shrugged. "Something dark, I suppose. Wasn't listening."

"Wasn't listening! He said something's coming to kill us!"

"Did he?"

Pierre tilted his head, one eye bigger than the other. He scanned the Cape as penguins drifted like careless fog.

"You don't actually believe him, do you?" Ferdinand asked, slapping Pierre's back. "They're the words of a bird trying to cling to what he had. Penguins will say anything when exile comes down on them, but you can't carry that stuff in your gizzard. Know how I know he was chocked full of guano?"

Pierre looked up from the sand.

"Why wait?" Ferdinand said, lifting his eyebrows "Why wait until you're about to be thrown out on your tail-feather to tell us we're in danger? A little convenient, don't you think? Could he have said something sooner?"

56

"I suppose," Pierre said.

"This was a bargain, a desperate one at that. Hoping if he gave us an extra special secret, we would let him stay. Which is utterly ridiculous."

Pierre's gaze panned the vacant plots of sand between domes. "Why couldn't he stay? There's space. Everyone deserves a second chance."

"If you knew our past, knew what he'd done, you'd reconsider. Here, we all depend on each other for food, shelter, medical aid, education, protection," Ferdinand explained, digging a hole with his foot. "If you're not helping us, you're hurting us. Stealing from hard-working citizens, living on their labor without giving anything in return, and this is what you become." Ferdinand removed his foot from the hole. "We fix it, or fall in." Ferdinand stepped back, wriggling his beak. "Solus has had more opportunities than there are letters in the word. It's time to go."

Ferdinand slid sand into the cone-shaped hole and tapped his foot, patting it smooth. Pierre stood, conflicted about how Caterwaul vacated its citizens, but understood why everyone needed to do their part. Having witnessed what happens to those who didn't, a decision had to be made.

The audience dispersed in clusters trudging to their designations. Adults to work and youth to the Academy. Not a soul went home and soon Pierre and his uncle were alone doing nothing which suddenly felt dangerous.

"You brought me here to show me the importance of getting a job."

"Work or walk. The Caterwaul way." He lifted a flipper. "Which, I think given your size, you'd be an excellent Preserver."

Pierre's eyes grew wide.

Ferdinand nodded. "Part of what those Emperors were doing. Monitor the shore and the sea, protect the residents, show out the unwanted. It's really a do-nothing job...until you have to do something."

Pierre looked down where six streaks marred the sand, three by each webbed foot of a penguin drug to his extinction. Pierre's stomach warmed. The thought kicked dust in his conscience. Everything he needed to know about a Preserver's duty was displayed moments ago.

Ferdinand and Pierre elected to consult with Patricia, and caught her as she was scurrying out of the boulder.

"D.E.W!" she shouted, running away. "Give your wounds time. Figure out what you want to do," she turned to backpedal, "good luck," she smiled. Faced with the ultimatum, vicious enforcer or mystery position, he took his aunt up on her offer. Trusting more her enthusiasm, than his familiarity with the strange acronym.

Ferdinand pointed Pierre in the direction of a dim cavern on the far side of the cape. Pierre stooped to fit under the passage, and was met by something small and energetic.

She spoke in rapid whispers. "Welcome to the cavern of the D.E.W. Are you dropping off or picking up?"

"Neither," Pierre said, matching her tone. "I'm here for a job."

She looked Pierre up, and down, and then back up. "As what, security? You're a little big to be a D.E.W. aren't you? Sure you don't want to be a Preserver?"

"Positive. I'd rather work here. My Aunt Patricia said it'd be good," Pierre said, not fully sure where *here* was, but figuring it must be better than *there*. He heard the term D.E.W. back home a few times in passing. He wasn't told what it was, but a lot of pretty penguins worked there and little more needed to be known.

"So *you're* the new one. There had to be one. The way they heaved Solus out of here like that."

Pierre was lost on how to process the statement. He cracked his beak to speak but words came out of hers. "After he'd been slacking this long I asked myself why now? You know? Why is this all of a sudden his judgment day?"

She looked at the wall, shaking her head and muttering. Then snapped back to Pierre. He blinked. She stepped to his stomach.

"But that's here nor there. So, you, o' leviathan seabird, would like to be a Designated Egg Watcher?"

A breath wheezed from Pierre as he heard the words. His jaw slipped ajar. *No bravado was to be found in this profession. I'm a Tee-Waddler*, he thought. *I should be courting soon, my potential mates will want to know what I do. I can't tell them I'm a big nanny*. He prattled over his words carefully, peering out of the cave.

He caught the little attendant smirk before she tucked it away. She stared at him daringly, leaning forward and grinning slightly. He refused to give her the satisfaction of him running, flippers flailing, screaming like a coward. The only way to maintain his dignity was to act as if he still had some.

He coaxed his composure and spoke with as much bass as his maturing voice could muster. "Yeah. I know penguins like me don't usually do this type of stuff but I figured it was about time to give these eggs some masculine tenderness."

They shared a long pause. It would have been better not to talk at all. She vacated his midsection.

"Hmph! If you're eager to serve then who am I? My name is Sherri, I'll show you what we do." Leading Pierre deep into a secluded inner section, she unveiled the backend of the cave.

A cocoon sprinkled with a few dozen eggs stretched a fourth of the total space. Some eggs white and oval-shaped, some yellow and more circular. Some metallic grey and others a faded burgundy freckled with splashes of neon green and obsidian.

"These are the future trouble makers of Caterwaul," she said. "Now what makes a good D.E.W. is a fierce attention to detail. You have to anticipate the needs of the penguin-to-be."

What needs? They didn't require a light jog, it was an egg. An egg that hadn't even hatched. It was an unhatched egg.

60

"Every so often you have to come back here and check their temperature. Place the back of your flipper on the median of the egg. If it's too warm, rotate it to a cooler plot. Too cold, warm it on your brood patch. Our life gives them life."

She paced the room, methodically nursing. She motioned for him to do the same. "The regulation of heat keeps them somewhere between liquid and ice." Sherri squeaked a cackle to her own dark humor as she shook her head and scooped a small lime colored oval onto her toe knuckles. Lifting her upper half, she slowly melted a warm bare patch of skin at the base of her stomach over the egg and relaxed.

"But seriously," Sherri continued, "there's nothing I love more than these eggs, especially with there being so few. This room used to be filled with all kinds of joy, left to right, I mean all kinds! But now, all we've got this corner. Which is why I guard them rabidly. No tolerance. You hurt my little chirp-chirps through intention, or neglect…and I'm comin'." She spied the new help. "You hear me. I'm comin'."

Pierre looked left, frowned, and nodded.

"Mmhmm," she said, "get warmin'. Third one second row is always a bit chilly."

Pierre relocated and sure enough it was frigid. He didn't have a brood patch since those mostly come with parenthood, but he mimicked her motions. When he got to a cold one he'd hunch over and give it a quick rub against his tummy until it was warm enough to set back down. He knocked a few over, accidentally sat his butt on others, and placed three or four upside down, but with repetition his blunders lessened. The two completed their rounds and returned to the front as the rising heat met them at the mouth of the cave. A glistening morning with warm wind and twinkling sand. The sweltering heat caused much fuss with his instructor and she griped as if she were suddenly dropped in this hot place today. After much talking and exacerbated sighs, she moved seamlessly into the gossip of the Cape—who chose who for the coming mating season, which ones really let themselves go, and who may be taking care of an egg that isn't theirs. Who's been talking mess and who's been doing it. Sherri required absolutely no response to hold full conversation.

Pierre deduced why some birds back home came here in droves. This place was a hotbed for all the wet gossip. A place where penguins could sit in the shade and barter speculation. He understood the appeal, but the hearsay earnestly had no draw on him. Shifting his focus to the outside world, he watched the sun intently. Hoping it'd hear his quiet plea. *Trudge faster. Please.*

Through the chatter, Pierre caught a glimpse of something like self-awareness.

"Am I talking too much? I hope I'm not talking too much. Do you think I'm talking too much? Because I don't think I'm talking too much."

Sherri continued to ramble. Pierre stood in the archway, invariably mute. Nothing to add, nothing to subtract, nothing to rebut, being slowly drained by endless noise.

She stood from her spot in the sand and finished a thought, "And she knew that wasn't his egg all along. I tell ya, that Bessie is Trifling 101. I'm going to the Reserve. Haven't been able to get to decent lunch since the last twelve assistants quit."

"*Twelve?*"

"Twelve. And ain't none of them worth a bit of nothin'. This used to be an operation. Overflowing. Guess these eggs were just too much for them. You can handle the rabble-rousers on your own for a while, right?"

Pierre nodded intensely.

"They won't bite. You want something? We've got Cod, Caper, Goby, Blenny, Smelt..."

Before Pierre could respond Sherri had talked her way down to the beach still naming fish.

Pierre stood at the edge of the cave, more relieved with each step she took. The day's sparkle was on the ocean. A warm breeze brushed across his face, reminding him so much of home. It wasn't hot outside, it was perfect. The heat luring him out of the cold. Pierre concluded, in that moment, he must escape. Slipping into the back room, with his plan, he gathered some eggs. Sooner than hoped, the sound of footsteps crunching sand echoed from the small entrance. He adjusted what he could and got into position.

Chapter 9

Marooned on this vaguely familiar island, Solus scraped cold collections of snow from his chest and wing. He felt a sharp burning sensation as he grazed the fresh gushing scars on his shoulders. The marks were mysterious, much like the penguins who put them there, but not understanding their translation didn't keep him ignorant of their meaning. He was the newest member of a group old as their civilization itself—the shunned, the unwelcomed, they who do not belong. Amongst the small band of cursed ex-citizens, purged from the place they call home, sworn to be killed on sight if ever they dared return.

Though the ever-present threat loomed over Caterwaul, for an actual Banishment to occur was rare. There were only four others like him that he could remember, three of which he heard had since moved on to the Celestial Nest, if such a place truly existed. Given the larger population, Solus was in small company.

Squinting, he surveyed the island, pestered with the strange inkling he'd been here before. To his left and right stretched a bare, unpainted Earth. A tundra colored only by passing reflections.

KING PENGUIN

Orange from the sun, light and dark blues from the ocean and sky, and white from the continuously falling snow. Some might make a mistake and call this place beautiful, but Solus saw it for what it was. The shades came and went, with the island having no control over when or how or why. Only vibrant under another's glow. Only illuminated in the presence of other light. No true shine. No color to call its own. Its true nature was hollow, and although Solus still wasn't sure if he knew this place, somehow, it reminded him of a smaller him.

Sand was the only thing his father stayed long enough to leave an impression on. Everything else went untouched. Solus spent more nights than his small mind could count standing on the doorsteps of the Atlantic, hoping the tide would wash in more than foam and knots of kelp. Seasons bled together as warm became hot, hot became cold, and cold became freezing. Somewhere in the midst of all that waiting and all that wanting, Solus stopped wishing. His hope hardened several times over as constant disappointment was sure to come as the rising sun. Absence nested instead of affection, and kindled a loathing to overthrow longing. Anger flourished with each passing year as he built his strength and started searching on his own, going farther and farther from the Cape. Looking no longer for love or warmth, that time passed, now he wanted something more appropriate. Retribution and revenge.

KING PENGUIN

The fiery orb up high burst through a gap in the clouds and lit up the ice as Solus glimpsed a tiny lump in the distance. Too small for a mountain and too large for a rock, curving up from the flat surface. The sun disappeared again as visibility was consumed by overcast and a flurry of snow. As always, the light was fleeting. Restricted and temporary, but darkness can be found anywhere, even in the height of day. There was value in this, he thought. The only thing trustworthy is consistency. Whether good or bad, at least he'd know what to expect.

Aligning with the vision in the distance, Solus punched his long, jagged claws into the hard ice for traction. Then, smiling wide, he marched.

Chapter 10

"What the flip are you doing!" snarled a husky voice.
Pierre gave a pleasant smile and wiggled in place. He shifted the
eggs around a bit. Adding some flare to his performance. Powerful
footsteps pounded around. Prickly pebbles of sand flung through
the air. This was better than he imagined. Keeping his eyes closed
was becoming harder to do. The temptation to peek was
overwhelming. Cracking a lid to enjoy Sherri's expression. What
he saw, however, was the physique of a robust Emperor mother. A
seething glare emanated from her dark violet eyes. She was bigger
than he was. Joy melted into fear. Pierre paused, blinking. *That's
not Sherri.*

"Get yo' fat head off my egg!"

That's not Sherri! Pierre rushed to his feet, apologizing,
stumbling, as the mother gripped her egg between the tips of her
wings and stormed out of the cave. Pierre followed her to the
archway desperately expressing his intention. The mother ignored
him, stomping down to the water's edge. Pierre watched as she

talked loud and aggressive to another penguin. Then, the two penguins on the shore turn and march toward the cave. Pierre pinned himself to the inside wall. Possibilities swam through his mind. He peeked around the corner. They were already much closer. He retreated to the back of the cave and started quickly rearranging his mess. The birds thundered into the room, and the mother placed her egg next to her in the sand.

"That's him!" the mother shouted.

Pierre swallowed so hard his beak clicked.

"He was using my Leviticus for neck support!"

"Pierre, is this true?" Sherri asked in her calmest tone of the day.

"Sort of, but I wasn't really. Just acting like it."

"Why?" Sherri asked.

"Because I thought it was you coming back to the cave."

"What difference does that make?"

"I wanted you to tell me I couldn't work here."

"You just got here!"

"I know."

"Why?"

"Honestly, you talk *a lot*."

Sherri glared at Pierre, shifted her weight and drew a deep breath.

"He ain't lyin'!" the mother cut in. "Sherri, you know you can talk. Beak run like the river. Flippity-flap-flap-flippity-flip!" The mother mocked, still frowning, then walked up close to Pierre. Her purple eyes were wide. A strained smile raised her cheeks high which made Pierre more uneasy. She laughed. Pierre did something of a laugh-shout in response. She stopped. Pierre stopped.

"Next time you want out of something you have two options: ask or use another egg. Last time we have this conversation. Mkay?" She brushed some sand from his shoulder.

He flinched.

Sherri bounced her focus between the two of them before settling on her employee.

"Why this hoopla? Why didn't you just quit?"

"I wanted to. I wanted to quit the minute I found out what a D.E.W really was. But I was embarrassed and didn't want to make it worse by being a coward or a quitter. This is a good job, but I need to be out there. So, for reasons you may not understand, and maybe I don't either, I need you to let me go."

Sherri paused and gave Pierre a look he couldn't quite read. "Get the hell out of my cave," she finally said.

"Thank you, Sherri. Thanks. I'm sorry." Pierre left. Pierre's bit of remorse disappeared like morning fog once he stepped into the sparkling sun. Whooshing waves, cawing gulls, walking penguins. His world came to life. He was never so happy to be fired.

Chapter 11

Finishing his first dip of the day, Paul Jaunty wiggled himself dry and waddled back toward his home. Reaching the entrance, he lingered in the archway with a wide stance. Paul drew a deep, satisfied breath relishing the reclaimed solitude of his home. He remembered crisply how much he felt like a complete hypocrite when he and his crew first came to Bouvet Island on an expedition.

As a Master Builder for his colony, Paul took pride telling his pupils if they could see it and scheme it, they could build it. If it was built in the mind, it could come to exist here. He'd given tons of lectures to students on creativity, problem solving, and using resources the land provided.

So, the irony then of a teacher unable to build anything in this place made him feel false. It made Paul feel as though he were a master of theory and motivational speeches only. All talk, but when things got tough, not good for much else. Paul wondered what happens when life gives you nothing to build with?

Struggling to build or find anything of value, they were flabbergasted when they discovered this dome, which sort of resembled a big off-white turtle shell. Not quite knowing what to do, the first wave of experiments was as follows: A penguin crept up to the dome. Squawked. Waddled away. Hid behind a small rock. Paul grinned. He remembered this particular experiment was attempted a total of thirty-six times.

After provoking the structure yielded no result, they moved to deeper studies. Testing the frame. The penguins pressed, prodded, and beat their wings along the outside of the dome. They listened closely for a shuffle or stir. Nothing. Progress was lethargic and likely would've remained that way until pure instinct revealed to them the purpose of this strange dome.

Caught in a vicious barrage of whipping frost and slicing wind, one of the many malicious snowstorms which visited this island, the penguins found themselves at a crossroads. With each passing moment, huddled tightly together on the open ice, they quickly became more fearful of the consequence of the rushing storm than whatever *could* be living in the dome. The five penguins bustled into the round space. And although an opening in the roof allowed some of the harsh storm in, they were still much better shielded.

Eventually, the storm passed. Roaring to terrorize another location. The small company of seabirds gingerly emerged from the circular space. As they turned to look back at the structure and witnessed the dome perfectly intact, its function became clear.

Convinced they needed something like this back home, Paul and his crew of penguins left the chilly island after that initial visit burning with hope and inspiration. They returned home and immediately went to work. Their extremely different environment presented many obstacles including: what to build with, how to build it, and who would help? Many penguins sized this task up as impossible. Even the hopeful admitted it was unlikely. But, Paul and his crew who were on the island that day didn't have the luxury of being disbelievers. Their very lives were saved by this thing. This wasn't fantasy, or something to keep them busy. This was important.

They searched their shores for building material. Which quickly turned out to be an empty pursuit. The beach was made of rocks which were too hard to shape and sand which was too soft to do anything with. Their noble project almost never made it off the ground. Until one day a treasury of talc was discovered by a penguin with an electric spirit for exploration whom Paul later grew very fond. Talc, the soft rock-like substance was perfect. Strong enough to support weight yet brittle to be trimmed, shaped, and even split using the beak as a chisel.

Thanks to the help of this citizen, Paul and his crew finally found their building material. The closest thing this sunny beach would get to blocks of compact snow and ice. 'What to build with' was solved. But *how to build it* was still a mystery.

Admittedly, at first, Paul and his team didn't know what they were doing. It had never been done before and much of what they tried was juvenile and base.

KING PENGUIN

As penguins, their bodies simply had limitations. They could trim and shape the rock-like substance, but surely couldn't lift it (or anything else) much higher than their gut. They needed some help.

Paul discussed the problem with the discoverer of talc, his new adventure-seeking friend. And, the next day, he couldn't find her anywhere on the Cape. Sneaking past the Safety's relatively new guards, Paul's friend slipped into the jungle and was gone for nearly two days. Paul feared he shouldn't have told her of his crew's problem. Paul had heard stories of the jungle and he worried dearly for her safety.

Yet, nearing sunset that second day, she returned. With help. Large, furry, help. Paul learned later that a kind of trade was made. The penguins would supply food to the large furry friends in exchange for their assistance. Initially, Paul was scared the penguins *were* the food, before learning they were friendly plant eaters. After a week of proving the penguins could collect enough leaves and plants to feed their large, hairy friends, the tree dwellers got to work.

Construction was now officially underway. The once beautiful and vacant beach now looked like a junkyard of strangely shaped white rocks. Workers laboring in other fields grew impatient with Paul's experiments. Disapproving of his crew's tests saying they didn't fall in line with the Cape's Contribution Clause. That this wasn't a contribution so much as a very stupid attempt which made a mess of their home.

But, over time, the crew's stubborn faith became infectious. As if working on and believing in this thing long and hard enough somehow made it important. Like seeing someone trying to accomplish a grand feat for no other purpose than to show to others it could be accomplished. The more the four devoted themselves to building this impossible thing, the more curiosity swirled around the event.

Questions rose around if penguins could really do something like this. Some bystanders offered help, others gave encouragement and others still their harsh opinion, but the group's resolve was growing with everything they learned. Every difficult step forward. There was a purpose for Paul and his crew being on that freezing island that day. A purpose for the storm. A purpose for the discovery.

For longer than Paul wanted to remember this attempt seemed foolish, ignorant, and out of touch with reality. Paul witnessed several near-complete collapses, domes which toppled pitifully in early stages, and others which stood for a day or two before caving for seemingly no reason at all. Through the series of failed attempts, the crew as best they could, tried to note the reason for their failure. Moving forward, as they tried not to not make the *same* mistake two and three times, one structure managed to stand.

KING PENGUIN

Unshaken by climate, passing time, or force. Paul's team, and other penguins, watched this experiment anxiously for many days.

Every day the structure remained standing was testament to what they'd accomplished. Proof that this truly could be done was erected in front of them. But, penguins were still very leery of its safety. So, Paul offered to move into the dome himself. To show his faith in the structure. He then offered he and his crew to build a dome for any who wished. Slowly, as one structure sprouted then endured, the new concept became more and more accepted until the very last penguins, still sleeping out on the open shore, came to Paul in private and asked if he and his crew would build their family a home. In the shadow of their success, the Cape was populated with many like structures.

The crew's achievement sparked an evolution in thinking from which Paul would never see the Cape digress. The inhabitants had seen what they knew a season ago to be purely impossible made possible.

The very first dome, the one Paul and his crew discovered that snowy, fateful day and hustled into during the stormy blizzard was the place Paul now inhabited. Paul named it 'Le Pere de Tous'. The shell which birthed all other shells.

The gap in the roof, which was largely seen as a structural flaw back home, was Paul's favorite part. He didn't care much for daytime. It was bright and bothersome. Haunting, in fact. But the night offered sparkles which shone into his circular space and made a bright bluish glow inside the dome. Paul loved it. He liked watching the constellations because he found them curious but more importantly, so he knew she was there.

In the twelve seasons since his adventure-loving partner passed, Father Time had yet to heal his wounds. The pain was still troublesome and violent and Paul hadn't made it far down the road to recovery. He shifted, in cycles, from anger to self-pity to self-loathing, back to anger. Lying on his slab staring through the northern void, Paul located the group of twinkling stars he sought. Paul exhaled thoroughly and his small frame sank.

Pyxis: the mariner's compass. She was his guide in this life and the next still the same. Paul's gaze never wandered far for long from the brief string of stars which reminded him of who he once was. When the freshness of the world hadn't yet started to fade, they would lie in the cool sand on a summer night. She'd point out star clusters with the number of little waddlers she wanted to have. Each star represented an egg. The first cluster she chose had fourteen stars. Paul remembered being quite nervous, waiting for a sign. A joke, a smile, a burst of her typical high-pitched laughter, or something. Something to show she was kidding. No signs came. Eventually, Paul discovered she was kidding. But that wasn't until much later. Paul figured in hindsight this was her way of making sure he was there to stay, no matter what.

After many polarized and comical debates the two settled on Pyxis. A cluster of stars which showed itself early that autumn, days before he and she were to be Bonded. Paul had a strange, private life rule. He never wanted more penguins than toes. He was thus thrilled to see the constellation Pyxis only had three stars.

His adventure-loving partner, who needed a way to contribute to the Cape while still quenching her thirst to see new places, became the colony's cartographer. Her mapping expeditions took her on explorations far from the settlement. Paul didn't know what to do when she was gone. He submersed himself in his work, laboring deep into the night. Building anything and everything he or anyone else could think of. When she returned home, her first order of business was to sketch everything from her journey into soft stone slate while it was still fresh in her mind.

Following one especially long trip, she couldn't stop talking about an enormous monster sitting on top of the water. Over time, the monster from her stories got closer until penguins could see it on the distant horizon from the beach's shore. It was a structure large and alien. Paul's partner spent plenty of time at sea, studying its form. Once home, she headed straight for her maps, marking her discoveries in great detail.

Each time she returned Paul noticed her feathers were a bit duller. A bit more colorless. Her beautiful black and white coat slowly became grey. The Medics said they'd never really seen anything like it before.

"It wasn't their fault. It *wasn't* their fault." Paul reminded himself. The Medics were accustomed to dealing with flesh wounds. Cuts and gashes from teethy predators but this was worse. It was killing her from the *inside*. Stealing everything except her life. And, eventually, it took that too.

That was it for Paul. He didn't care about building anymore. It was stupid. He didn't care about the Cape. The penguins were a nuisance. He saw reminders of their time together in every detail of the wretched place. Early one morning, without warning, his vision blurred with tears, Paul left the colony and once again sought shelter here.

Paul slipped off his slab and waddled across the room. In front of him now was a series of arcs and curves he made with his beak, neatly sculpted into the wall. The lines came together to form the portrait of a beautiful Adelie. An elegant mural, seen best by the glow of starlight. Crooning his neck, Paul carved some corrections. Touching the ice, he mourned for their broken connection.

Suddenly, the light disappeared from the doorway and a voice crawled into Paul's ear. "She's beautiful," it said, lingering just beyond the arch.

Paul quickly spun around. What crept in from the darkness was tall and scarred. Its eye sockets were sunk far back into its skull and it's beady eyes, the size of pebbles, shone with a blood-red radiance. The combination made looking into his eyes like staring down the vent of a volcano.

Paul staggered backwards. "Ravillac!"

"Oh, Professor. Must we be formal? Call me Solus."

Chapter 12

Tiberius Flock could never forget the night Patricia hired him. "I need an albatross to do something dangerous," she said, peering down at him in the pale moonlight. The logical response would have been a spike of curiosity followed by thoughtful questions: what she needed him to do, what made it dangerous, and why she didn't do it herself. Tiberius wondered even then was she only asking because she felt he was disposable? This way, if everything went south they could be happy they didn't lose someone *really* important? Those were the questions Tiberius felt he should've asked. The thought process he should've worked through but instead he said nothing. Nothing but "absolutely." The question wasn't even a question to be answered in the negative or affirmative, in fact it wasn't even a question at all, but he didn't care. He wanted her to know, whatever, however, he was her bird.

A chance to work for one of the most influential birds in Caterwaul was a chance to upgrade his place in the caste system. This position brought notoriety, status, and pride. Things, at the time, he knew nothing about. He would no longer be just an albatross, he would be *Patricia's Trans-Atlantic*. That meant something. And the blind risk seemed small compared to the certain misery he would endure if he'd continued living as an awkward oaf good for nothing more than entertainment. He could never outrun the sneers of his critics and bullies who would never ever accept him as their equal. As an orphan, a normal life wasn't an option. Each visitor who had come to see that year's batch of parentless albatross sighed and looked upon him with such pity he felt pity for their pity.

By nightfall first day, his only remaining company were the sick and injured at birth. He resolved, eventually he would be shooed away with the others. Until, one night she walked up so quietly, for a moment, he didn't even know she was there. She was average height and very quiet. She didn't say anything to him when he noticed her. Silently, she pointed to his wings. He stretched them for her to see, far and wide until he could barely hold them up. She motioned with her chin for him to go run. Tiberius took four steps, wobbled, and tipped over. She elongated her neck, signaling him to caw. What resonated was a shrilled yip, like nails on rock. She smiled. Still not saying a word.

Tiberius thought on this while flying across the ocean as the rushing wind parted at the tip of his beak. He'd just finished delivering the news to Pierre's parents in the Falklands and was now en route home to Caterwaul. Tiberius wondered what it would be like if he said no that odd night. He envisioned his future like walking the endless dark corridor of a dripping cave. If he couldn't make it as a Messenger he had no place in the Cape.

Though he could fly long distances, he wasn't a very quick sprinter, and had no talent for extraction. The only other role an albatross could offer value to Caterwaul and its citizens. Patricia gave him what no one else would: a right to be there. A right to their home. A right to stay. Without which, he would be very much like Solus.

Chapter 13

After successfully annoying a collection of Humboldt penguins chiseling rocks on the shore, Pierre learned Patricia's location. She was somewhat well-known, before Pierre described what she looked like, the birds called her by first name and pointed impatiently down the beach. Pierre wandered through the mouth of a circular gaping hollow, far into the mountainside, passing Patricia's face, five times that he could count, scratched into both sides of the wall. Dramatic profiles of her, chin lifted, gazing into the distance. He approached the sixth one where below the inscription read: Patricia Oiseau – Safety of the Cape.

Pierre fathomed this Academy was similar to theirs back home. A place the young came for general education before being assigned a specific career. Though the curriculum here surely had to be different. While Pierre suffered through war strategy and combat training in the Falklands, here, they might learn stone shaping or, eesh, egg nurturing. Pierre shuddered. The inside of the cave was on a mild slope, and pools of water collected when the tide was high enough to wash in. The stationary water chewed holes into the rock causing small, pumpkin-shaped cavities. Pierre ventured over to peer inside of one of the curious rooms when a rumble echoed through the hallway. Something was coming, running, splashing, shrieking. Pierre swung around just in time to see floods of Wee-Waddlers filling the width of the cave pouring out of their prisons, rushing toward him. Screaming as they rushed around him, bumbling toward the beach. Pierre watched the jubilant masses as they paid him virtually no attention on their way to the sunshine.

His aunt trailed the horde, looking mildly surprised to see him standing there like a rock in a rushing stream.

"Sherri?" she asked, walking slowly.

Pierre nodded guiltily.

"Figures. She could talk through her own funeral. Nobody can stand it for too long, but I was hoping you'd at least make it through the day. For your wounds."

"I'm fine," Pierre responded, looking down and off. Patricia jabbed him with a stiff poke. Pierre forcefully cleared his throat. She circled around the green bandages and lanced him with another. It would've hurt if he was injured or not. *How was she so strong?* Pierre winced while she was behind him but held a straight face when she was back in front.

"See," he gritted. "Healed."

His aunt let out a startling bright laugh. "Impressive then! Sherri healed you in half a day. We should put her in the Wellness Ward."

"I don't know," Pierre said, wanting to say more but not wanting to be mean.

"Sherri is irregular but she provides a valuable service. Not many have the patience to sit all day coddling the unhatched. If it weren't for her, a lot of us would not be free to do what we do."

"Yeah," Pierre said, not fully convinced.

"If you had to be in a dark and lonely cave all day you would sniff out things to entertain yourself too. Now come, we have something to discuss."

Patricia motioned toward the opening, led Pierre out and watched her students. As the two moved further closer to the beach, crunching of sediment mixed with the giggles of youth at play.

"You've been through a lot at your age," Patricia said, walking in slow, deliberate steps. "Our more…troubled pupils here at the Academy could benefit from your experience. To help them make sense of their own lives and some of the things that have happened. I was thinking today, it could be beneficial for everyone if you spent time as a counselor. These students are at such a transitional age, they won't be Wee Waddlers much longer. Soon they'll be in the thrust of adolescence and you coming out of the phase they're about to enter might offer something to help them on their way."

Pierre pondered his aunt's words. A breeze brushed across his face as Pierre smelled the sea. Then, suddenly a shadow swept overhead. Patricia brayed twice and Tiberius dropped with a boom and explosion of sand at her side. This was the first time Pierre got to see the bird up close. The immaculate albatross had a white chest of neatly groomed feathers that transitioned into cherrywood wings and a dark golden beak. Tiberius fluttered and tucked his wings, then he and Patricia started their incessant whispering. Patricia laughed something into his ear. The albatross half-turned to Pierre, shook his head, and turned back. It didn't take telepathy to know Pierre's theatrics would soon be Trans-Atlantic news. His mother may chuckle about the eggs but his father would find no humor in it at all. Pierre felt the cold paternal stare across the ocean. His parents risked a lot, including their livelihood, to get him to safety and repaying it with immature shenanigans was beyond explanation.

Patricia walked up to Pierre's side and nodded to Tiberius as he rocketed into the air. The sudden gust pushed Pierre back in the sand but Patricia stood firm.

"Made a decision?" she asked, turning around to her nephew.

Pierre stepped forth. He understood her rationale and the concern for her students, but how could *he* lead anyone? What did he have to offer? He was new. He didn't know anything, or anyone much at all, and wasn't *great* at anything. What's worse, he was a temporary fixture in this new world. And would leave as swiftly as he came if ever called home. Was it wrong to forge this trust and build these relationships, presenting himself as someone they could count on when his being here was so fickle? In his gut, he didn't feel quite ready or qualified to lead others or give life advice. Pierre blew air into his cheeks, held it there, and then let it out.

"Well, I won't force you," his aunt stepped in. "But know when you're ready, you have something special many of us could use. I understand right now may be too soon, but don't wait forever. You're more than an *ex*-Egg Watcher," she smiled. "In the meantime, if you're any good on the chase you can try your luck at your old job."

Pierre frowned. "How do you know about my old job?"

Patricia donned an omniscient grin. "A birdie told me. But, if you're going, you'd better hurry. The sun is already at its peak, roll call will start soon. If it hasn't already."

Pierre pivoted quickly to face the sea, ablaze with a new energy. "Let me help you out," his aunt said, nipping the end of his stale seaweed and unraveling him in circles. "You don't want them thinking you're a liability."

Stumbling to regain his balance, Pierre gathered his bearings and scurried off toward the beach.

"They'll have a hard enough time trusting you as is," Patricia muttered to herself, watching her brother's son bumble toward the glistening sea.

Chapter 14

Solus slowly circled the inside of the dome. He carefully eyed Paul's possessions: withered flowers, stones from the sea, and a pile of neatly laid kelp. Paul silently tottered in place, afraid to pause the intrusion of his own home. Solus' jagged claws slid back and forth across the ice.

As the Fiordland slithered near a certain spot on the wall, Paul found the courage to speak. Usually a brave, rambunctious bird, he could recall the last time he was this nervous. "What are you doing here Ra…umm…Solus?" Paul patted the edge of his beak.

"Searching."

"For what?"

"Answers."

"To what?"

"The questions I haven't learned to ask."

Solus' cryptic response did little to settle Paul or clear the confusion. Three years had gone by since Paul had seen the bird pacing his home. Solus held a distant and disturbing nature even when he was his pupil at the Builder's Academy. To be accepted into Paul's department, students had to display superior cognition in the fields of intellect, motor skill, and interspecies communication during their time at the Academy. Paul's requisites were nonnegotiable, and he made no exceptions. Constructing a living environment was a beautifully dangerous task. Caterwaul was one of the few places he heard of bold enough to even try it. He wanted to be sure they were properly qualified and respected the risk.

Paul took his students to Bouvet Island several times throughout the year to study this very structure and apply this ancient wisdom to their forms back on the Cape. Paul was stiff, and had his favorites, but was always fair. The potential price of mistakes made Paul impatient to error. One piece out of place, one block not chipped perfectly to form, and an entire dome could crash with the family sleeping inside. It was an honor, not a right to build and most students were so anxious, yearning to join the elite group of penguins who would literally build a better tomorrow, they couldn't sit still while Paul delivered the news. But, Solus was different.

When Solus bothered to stop by Paul's outdoor lectures, he sat closest to the ocean, quietly fixed on the never-ending sea. Whenever class was held in the cave, he arrived but left soon after, often while Paul was in the middle of lecturing. There was no way of knowing for sure how much information Solus retained because whenever Paul asked him a question in class, Solus would toss back a question of his own.

KING PENGUIN

How many builders does it take to assemble a structure? *How many does it take to pull it apart?* What are the strengths of using a thirteen-stone base system? *What are its weaknesses?* Why are we, as Builders, important to the colony? *Why are these citizens important to us?* And so it would go every session Paul happened to be vexed with Solus' presence. Paul encouraged the desire to attain information, but secretly grew to loathe Solus' defiant curiosity.

"Any visitors lately?" Solus asked, breaking Paul's train of thought.

"Why do you ask?"

"I noticed this dent here in this kelp. Only a shape like yours could make such a small, wide hole, so I thought, that's strange. Why not sleep here..." he pointed to the slab in the center of the room. "...where you were meant to sleep? Why in the corner of your own home?"

"Well, sometimes I—"

"No, no. That wasn't a question." Solus paused, still and rigid, examining his old professor. Paul felt Solus' red gaze trickle across every inch of his being.

"When I entered, I saw a different kind of indentation here on the bed, than the kelp over there. Something quite larger than yourself, then I became curious. So, I'll ask again. Have you, Paul, had any visitors lately?"

KING PENGUIN

Paul tried to guess what Solus could possibly want with that information. Or why he cared. Yet, while Paul couldn't decipher his motives or reasoning, one thing was certain—Solus wasn't planning to do *anything good* with this knowledge.

Paul stole a glance at the raw engravings carved into each of his wings, shocked he hadn't focused on them before. Deep markings revealing white and red flesh meat with scar tissue bubbled to the surface. That's when it struck him, Solus was not away from the colony by choice. Those marks of banishment meant Solus was more than just odd or disturbed, more than cruel or vindictive; he was also desperate. A bird with no home, out here in this cold, harsh, nothingness was a bird waiting to die. Paul knew that better than anyone. But why did he come *here*? Did he come to take this dome from me for shelter? Put me out of my home? If so, why the questions, why the pauses, the show, why not just get to it? Paul felt a wave of warm impatience roll over him.

Solus paced again moving toward a specific spot on the wall. Paul shifted.

"Just an old friend," Paul finally said, louder than he intended. "A pal from an island over come to pay me a visit. Nothing fancy. Look if it's the dome you need we can just share it."

Solus pivoted quickly, bent his neck forward, then smirked. "A friend...from an island over...come to pay you a visit." The words rolled out slowly. Then, Solus let out a chuckle which sounded like

90

a growl. "You were a hopeless recluse even before you lost your poor Felicia."

"Flora." Paul tensed, correcting him. There were few things Paul was afraid of, and death, ironically, was something he developed a conflicted longing for; but this was different. This didn't feel like *his* life on the line. Solus had no cause or vendetta against him. No reason to go through this trouble, to seek him out after all this time. True, Paul had Solus removed from the Builder's Program, recommending him for a different position. But Paul earnestly felt he was doing him a favor, giving Solus more time with the only thing he seemed truly interested in. The sea. Paul shook his head softly in thought, peering down at his icy floor. If Solus were here for revenge or take Paul's home from him they would've been tussling already. Paul recognized he was being manipulated for purpose. What purpose? He couldn't be sure.

Solus crumpled his vibrant yellow brows as if trying to look directly through Paul. "Flora, yes, of course, forgive me but I was offended. A friend from an island over," Solus scoffed. "You can do better." Solus touched the slab in the center of the room. "Bouvet is the most popular resting stop for travelers going in and out of the Cape. When the Great Excavation isn't underway, this island is a funnel for all things heading into the 'greatest colony on Earth'." Solus echoed the words with rage through the circular gap in the roof. "As a mapmaker's widower I expect you know this. If any new bird went into that Cape it would've come through here.

91

So, for a friendless, loveless, sad, loner, such as yourself to claim you've had visitors is very, *very* insulting," Solus grumbled, clamping his beak, stepping closer. "No one visits you. No one stops by. No one drops in. Just me. Just now."

Paul's soft back was pressed against the cold wall. Highlighting the massive size difference between him and Solus. Flush against the mural of his lost wife, Paul gasped in the shadow of the towering frame. Paul's strength wavered.

"Professor," Solus scowled, speaking down at the top of Paul's head. "I crave your knowledge. Tell me who you've been harboring. Tell me why you are lying for them. Why you are keeping them from me, and I'll be on my way."

Sliding his foot back an inch, Paul felt the thud of his heel hitting the solid wall. Nowhere to go. Entering the physical prime of adulthood, Solus was faster and stronger than the aging professor in every way. Paul stilted the quiver in his body. Turned his head to the side. The side of his face brushed Solus' chest. Paul swallowed the tremble in his voice. Then, parted his beak. "A friend," he said again, barely above a whisper.

Solus quickly stepped back. His fiery eyes shot back and forth across Paul's face in every which direction. Paul felt Solus calculating. Reading him. Every response. Every twitch. Every squint. Every flinch. Solus crooked his neck, peering behind Paul. Solus stared for a moment at the curious wall behind Paul. Then spun and marched toward the door.

"Let's try this another way," Solus raged, throwing the words back over his shoulder. "Remember your lecture on cornerstones? Let's test that theory."

The blood left Paul's face as Solus vanished into the dark.

Chapter 15

Was it safer to be inside the dome or out? Solus' parting remark lingered like a dark foretelling of things to come. The irony of course was that this was a domed structure. Thus, there were technically no corners or cornerstones, which would be good, except not having a cornerstone actually made every base block of equal importance. This is the point Paul made to his students on the importance of precision in cutting and laying your stones. You could remove any block along the bottom row and collapse a home. The silence was taunting. Outside was still. Paul wasn't convinced of any deep breaths or quick motions. The small bird dreamt a quick dream that it all went away. That his interrogator decided he was telling the truth.

It was silly. Nearly every known colony sleeps on their webbed feet in the shifting elements, while the seabirds of Caterwaul graduated to shelter. Other colonies filled their day with base survival, each family for his or herself. Caterwaul managed a division of labor. Progressions in leaps, born from the notion that some do stuff better than others and should concentrate on that for the benefit of all. Departments were created to nurture intellect, kindle potential, and capitalize on skill, for the better of all. Simply living became extinct. Schools restructured to teach more than how to catch food and how to avoid being it. With this breakthrough, they lusted for a deeper understanding of themselves and the world around them. How to fix a sick body, overcome limitations, and make the most of what else is out there. They prodded and poked and probed and pushed and grew and swelled and grew. Never stopping to think how much more dangerous a dangerous penguin could be once educated. How, if knowledge is power, and power can corrupt, then education is the key to massive destruction. How increasing the tools for good, increases tools for the opposite. How light gives birth to shadow.

Boooom!

The powerful sound of pounded against the wall of the dome. Paul swung around to the point of impact as the deafening rumble thundered in the hollow space. *Boooom! Boooom!* The sound bounced off the walls and howled up into the night's sky. A sharp glitch on the far side of the room caught Paul's peripheral. He rushed over. Solus was hitting the stone below Paul's portrait of Flora. The image twitched, slipping inch by inch with every thumping blow. Paul trembled. His throat tightened and his gut turned searching for a solution. Solus was willing to collapse the building with him in it if he didn't tell him what he wanted to know.

KING PENGUIN

Paul pressed his body up against the mural, trying to push back the smooth piece that was coming out. The glistening ice gave no traction as his claws slipped and scraped with each knock. *Bam! Bang! Bam! Bam! Bam! Pock!* The block popped loose, as a jailbreak of cold air rushed in through the void. The shapes above miraculously collapsed to fill the space as the entire side unsteadily slumped. Paul stepped aside as the dislodged block slid past him to the center of the room. Then, the sound jumped back to life as Solus continued.

Paul had to go, he knew he had to, but he couldn't do it. He couldn't forsake her. It was just a picture, an image he scratched into the dome with his claws and beak, but it was all he had. Watching her die twice was more than he could do.

"Tell me who was here!" Solus screamed through the wall. "Tell me! Who took my place! Give me a name!" With every muffled directive came a vicious slam. A second block sprung free, as the slam of blocks falling into a random order charged through the room. The structure buckled, that entire wall wavering with the running wind.

"There's nothing to tell!" Paul yelled.

"Tell me!"

Boom!

"Please! Solus!"

"Tell me!"

Boom!

"Don't do this! I'm begging you!" Paul cried as he touched his Flora. The portrait shook and rattled against his flipper. Paul's soft words drowned in the onslaught.

"Tell me!" Solus shouldered another block from the foundation. Flora's face became misshapen, warped, uneven. Something warm and wet dripped down Paul's cheek.

"Please," Paul sniffed. "Please. I love her."

Paul noticed he was no longer yelling. Barely talking above a normal tone to himself. The noise never stopped. Paul looked wearily up into the night sky up at Pyxis. The rumbling dome moaned, threatening to give way. How it lasted this long was nothing short of an amazing mystery. He took a last assessment of the structure. This was it. The dome had compensated all it could. It wouldn't survive another lost block. Perhaps this was for the better, Paul thought. Perhaps Solus was his relief. Someone to excuse him from a life he'd long stopped living. An undertaker, well overdue, come to collect his shell.

One memory ran in his thoughts. Embers of a fear Paul could never force himself to forget. The overwhelming helplessness he felt when the Sickness was coursing through his Flora. How he gazed at her, stuck and powerless. He wished over and over he could get rid of that feeling. That guilt. Wishing he could go back and play a more significant part in that outcome. That he could've made it different. Oddly, he had a choice in this moment. Some portion of power or control over her future. This time he could save her. Or at least her image. His brain raced through questions.

Why was he risking his home and the mural of the only one he loved for a penguin he barely knew? Why was he enduring this for Pierre? Was it for Pierre? Was he punishing himself? Was it because he knew, against his will, Flora's time had passed and he needed to let her go? Was it because part of him wanted this? To leave this world and join her in the Celestial Nest? Or was it because he felt it meant a death sentence to give Solus any name he felt linked to his banishment? Paul really didn't know.

He surveyed what was left of his crippling sanctuary and his mate. She was ugly now. Solus made her ugly. He gazed at the massive destruction that had been done. He shook his head furiously.

"What could Solus possibly want this badly with Pierre?"

The words crept out barely above a whisper. Then, suddenly, it stopped. *Impossible.* His internal ears were ringing in the new silence. He could barely hear himself think over the relentless pounding, let alone speak.

Pierre heard Solus panting heavily. He was close on the other side of the slumped wall. Then, Solus' breathing ceased. When strength returned to Paul limbs he stumbled outside. Solus was nowhere to be found.

Chapter 16

Tripping twice en route, Pierre sloshed to a stop next to four birds in line. Each stood stiff as a tree, and Pierre could tell preliminary detail had already started.

A Chinstrap with narrow eyes and square jaw stomped back and forth in front of the group punching small potholes into the sand. Starting with someone at the far end, he issued commentary on yesterday's expedition.

"Xander! You're faster than a Tiger shark late for work. Which is why I let you be Spear opposite me on the hunt. But accuracy comes from control, and knowing when to use that speed. Time your attacks. Be in sync with your team. Your giddiness is costing us catch. Last chance."

Xander nodded hard, adjusting his posture, making it straighter than it already was. Pleased with the silent compliance, the leader moved down the aisle. Pierre nudged the Magellanic penguin to his right. Pierre nudged him once. He didn't move. Twice. No response. The third time, Pierre nudged him into a brief stumble. The penguin peddled back into place and shook his head.

KING PENGUIN

Their Sachem stopped in front of a tall bird with the figure of a teardrop.

"Puddles! I don't know how many times I have to tell you! Our job is to catch for the colony. Not eat in their place. Yet ev-e-ry time we go out, you bring back more fish in your gut than you do with your beak! You've been a Straggler since you started, and today, nothing will change."

Pierre bent forward enough to see Puddles smirk and shrug when the Sachem wasn't looking.

"Aria!" The commander barked. "Beautiful execution. Incredible technique. Improve your jousts, and you can have Xander's spot up front."

"Yes, Sachem," her voice replied to the commander in a clear, soft tone.

Pierre leaned again to take a look. The Sachem shot him a swift glance and Pierre snapped back.

"Cole! Great work. You're a reliable bird. I have nothing more to say," the Sachem said to a boxy Galapagos penguin before stepping in front of Pierre.

Gazing at his cast, he bent sideways and whispered low, "I want you to know you are not slick. You are not sly. I don't know who you are."

"I'm—"

"Couldn't care less. I want to tell you the last bird who took this job let us all down. So, you could have the experience of an unhatched egg and be slow as a manatee in mud but you better be loyal. You *better* be loyal. You abandon this team and you can forget about Banishment. I will stuff you into the jaws of an Orca myself."

Pierre sprung a shocked look into the Sachem's dark brown eyes, hoping for banter or farce but only found a discomforting sincerity.

"Don't worry," Pierre responded. "I couldn't leave if I wanted to." In that moment, Pierre felt a rush of anger toward his parents.

The soft matter of the commander's face scrunched in the middle. It was now a compact clump of features, glaring at Pierre. "Good," the commander finally said. Appearing to be coming off his edge a bit, he looked Pierre up and down. "Good."

Chapter 17

A breeze swished over Pierre as the Sachem quickly stepped away. The stout Chinstrap waddled waist deep in the water and gazed at the horizon. The other four assembled into position. Two were diagonal rear-right to the Sachem, one diagonal rear-left, and one in the middle. The form resembled a tilted "4." Pierre plugged into the last spot on the back left, completing the "A" formation and sighed.

Half a body in the sea, the Sachem peered into the tumbling waves. Lingering in what seemed like a meditative trance, the calm tide pushed him back and forth, before he shouted.

"Xander, patience. Wranglers, make that noose furious. Stragglers, be ready for the burst!"

Puddles was across from Pierre and shot him a curious glance as if just noticing he was with them. His belly hung low as he inched toward the surf.

The high noon sun churned to its summit as the six members leaned forward above the low water.

"Caaaatccchhhers!" the Sachem barked. "A-tta-que!"

KING PENGUIN

The group splashed into the Atlantic surf without breaking form, swimming at a rapid pace just below a sprint. Being at the back of the brigade meant Pierre was a Straggler. A job he spent a great deal of time trying to get promoted from back home. With the expedition now underway, his time for protest had passed.

Bubbling through the Epipelagic, the pointed arrow of underwater jet streams riffled far away from the coast. Each penguin shadowed the Sachem's moves with only split-second delay. They sifted through green sea forests and rainbow-shaded reefs. They swam past many collections of trout, skipper, and silverfish, and Pierre began to have budding doubts about their commander's senses.

Pierre noticed a strange melodic hum grew louder and louder as they gurgled past hordes of food. *What was that sound?* The catch grew scarce as they burst through an obscure pocket of what looked like a grey cloud under the water. Pierre was temporarily blinded as the group exited out of the bottom out of the last strange, grey, underwater cloud, and the team sank into a shimmering circular gorge. It was a small colorful canyon. With types of fish Pierre could recognize and many he'd never seen before. The team adjusted their angle. Now swimming toward the surface moving at full speed. Pierre scrambled to catch pace as Xander swiftly moved level with the Sachem. They shot through the water's surface in teams of twos, Xander-Sachem, Aria-Colt,

Pierre-Puddles. Six glistening bodies sprang up into the South African sunlight.

As he rose into the air, Pierre heard the Sachem's voice in the ruffling wind.

"Wranglers! Fall out!"

Colt and Aria in the second tier keeled over and sliced back into the ocean, splitting in different directions once they hit the water. Xander and Sachem followed suit, falling like arcing tears along the outsides of the still rising Stragglers. Pierre and Puddles turned last, and dropped themselves back in.

Back underwater, Pierre could see Aria and Colt swirling a thunderous turbine around the biggest collection of fish he'd seen. *Zyoom! Zyoom! Zyoom! Zyoom!* Quicker and quicker and quicker. Assuming the role of Master Spear, the Sachem rose above the trapped circle of fish as his partner dropped below. Taking turns, they shot through the consolidated mass, picking off doubles and triples before returning to the surface lofting the catch up to a circling flock of albatross. Pierre stared through the watery window to the action above. One by one, blurry white birds filled their beaks and darted off back toward the colony.

The Wranglers, Colt and Aria, circled the fish tighter and tighter, backing them closer and closer to the middle. Soon, they were too thick to pass through. Spears halted their attack as Pierre and Puddles waited along the extremities. Once the Spears stopped shooting through the fish, the Wranglers accelerated, circling faster and faster at a blinding speed. The shimmering globe of fish had small implosions, like a giant twitching orb. The equator shrunk. The prey crowded into the center until no more space was left at the core. Then, the fish stopped as Pierre and Puddles bobbed with the current. The Sachem rose a flipper, paused, and dropped it.

A brilliant flash of silvery scales exploded in every direction, bursting into the bluish ocean. The fish raced in a stricken fury as Pierre steadied himself in the rushing stampede. He leaned. Snapped. Spun. Jousted. Twisted. Lanced. Twirled. Clamped. Snatching everything he could before lofting it to the albatross circling above then slicing back into the ocean. Soon, with the albatross not being able to make the trip to shore and back quickly enough, whatever Pierre lobbed into the air fell back into the ocean.

On the other side of chaos, Pierre managed to catch a glimpse of Puddles nibbling patiently at whatever swam by. Possibly capturing one for every twelve that bounced off his face. Twice Pierre saw him start toward the surface, stop halfway, and swallow what he caught.

Docking on the Cape, the crew wiggled themselves dry. Aria, Colt, Puddles, and Xander sprinted down the shore and Pierre followed suit. They stopped at the Reserve almost crashing into one another as they stopped and stretched their neck up at the massive pile of fish. Six albatross were leaning against the catch, heaving breaths. A mountain of wet, wiggling bounty spilling out of the Reserve.

"FOR-mation!" the Sachem shouted, walking up behind the group. He opened his beak then closed it shut. He raised his flipper, then put it back down at his side. He stood in front of Pierre. Huffed. Stared. Squinted.

"You are obscure."

Pierre heard Xander whispering something down the aisle.

"Don't bother counting them Xander," the Sachem said, not removing his focus. "You're wasting your time."

Xander frowned and broke formation walking over to the fish. He slapped a corner of the pile. A small avalanche of fish slid in its place. "Looks can be deceiving," Xander said.

"Yes. If you don't know what you're looking for," the Sachem countered, ignoring Xander's blatant insubordination.

"This might not be what it seems!" he squealed.

"Yes," the Sachem said, eying Pierre like a dazzling gem.

"How do we know it's enough?"

"Cause I've been counting catch since before you were rattling around in your mama's gut! Cause I know the eating habits and volume of every bird in this colony! Cause there is a *reason* I am the Sachem! It's enough! So Xander shut your Chub hole and get back in line!" the commander snapped, finally giving Xander his full attention.

106

Aria, Colt, and Puddles giggled and shoved each other as the commander switched back to staring at Pierre with little regard for his individual space.

Circling Pierre, the Sachem mumbled. He mumbled and circled. Circled and mumbled. Circled some more. Mumbled some more. Until he made a small, empty moat around Pierre.

"What the..." He poked Pierre's side. Pierre squirmed. "Lookin' like..." the Sachem said. He slapped belly. Pierre winced, then stood back straight. "With the...HMPH...I tell you what!"

The Sachem wasn't making sense. Pierre wasn't sure if he was in trouble.

"There's enough here to feed the colony, the albatross, and Puddles." Puddles leaned forward, looking down the aisle. "Back in line!" The commander shouted. Puddles stood straight.

"We're done," the Sachem snapped suddenly. "Disperse!"

The group was hesitant to move. The group eked away in different directions but soon ended up following Pierre. They were walking several steps behind him like he was a strange creature they were stalking. Pierre turned around. They each looked into the distance. There was an awkward period of silence. Then one of them spoke.

"You hunt good!" Puddles said.

"*I* hunt good," Aria corrected, "but what is the word for *this*?"

"Mediocre," Xander said as he pushed his way through the three of them. "Anyone can have one lucky day on the catch."

Aria smirked. "You've *never* been that lucky."

"I have."

"Have not."

"Have too."

"No-you-have-not!"

"I would've remembered," Puddles offered with a hint of authority.

"He just snatched the scraps I left behind," Xander scoffed.

Aria huffed. "A lot of scraps."

"Tasty scraps," Puddles added.

"Whatever! We can't go around getting excited because some penguin we don't even know brought back a couple extra."

Aria pointed to the towering pyramid. "It's three times the daily catch, and there would've been more if the albatross could've kept pace."

"I don't blame the albatross. I blame his sloppy technique."

Puddles' face scrunched like he bit into something sour. "Ouuu ou ou! The ocean ain't the only thing salty."

Aria laughed. "Xander, get over yourself. I don't know how you see it, but this is a good thing."

Puddles turned to Pierre, his fellow Straggler. "Where'd you learn to do this?"

Pierre shook loose from a distant gaze, "Um."

Xander started prancing in place. "Oh, where'd you learn it," he mocked Puddles with a poor imitation. "It doesn't matter where he learned it! We can't trust him. And that's the bottom line. The only thing that matters. You all remember last time we had a 'too-good-to-be-true' Catcher? You saw how that turned out. He left. For days at a time. Gone. Leaving us to starve. Remember? Our catchers couldn't keep up because demand had gotten too big. A lot of penguins didn't make it through the famine. So, if he really is everything you think he is, the only question that really matters is how do we know we can trust him? How do we know we can depend on him? How do we know he'll be there when we need him?"

A hush came upon the gathered. The Cape's lunch break was now underway, and every bird within an earshot drew into the congregation. Bundles of penguins and albatross from different professions gawked at the pile on the shore.

Pierre's chest sunk a little. "Xander's right. I don't know how long I'll be here." Groans rumbled from those who were listening. Xander grinned, as the crowd began to turn. "But I do know how it feels to be hungry. I know how it feels, in bad times, to share a single fish between four penguins, hoping it gets you through the night. I know how it feels for a place to lose penguins they love when it didn't have to be that way. I don't know what I can promise. I don't know if this is luck like Xander says. But what I can promise is that while I'm here, I'll do everything I can to make sure you never have to feel the way you've felt again."

The audience roared. The slapping of wings clashed with the sound of dozens of seabirds braying into the air. More penguins trickled down toward the shore as Preservers rushed in, alarmed. In clusters, they came and came and came until more than half were there.

This good news spread faster than gossip. As one citizen relayed to another and another the details became more and more and exaggerated. The legend of Pierre's promise was greater than the promise itself. He saw penguins pointing to the mountainous pile in the Reserve, enough for a colony more than twice their size, to convert skeptics slow to believe this new, unknown King penguin could make good what they heard.

The citizens swiftly decided, with Pierre none the wiser, that the hatching limitations would be lifted. One egg per household was no longer was necessary. They could now provide enough food to grow a bigger colony. Have bigger families. And replace some of the life they lost. The Cape was eager. On the cusp of the mating season, the news could not be better.

Chapter 18

Patricia heard the news later that evening of her nephew's declaration. The Cape more vibrant than she could ever remember. Caterwaul's daily sunset swim went much longer than usual, extending long into the moonlight. Citizens were kinder and more patient. Builders spent extra time chiseling keepsakes and sculptures. Patricia's adopted home now brimmed with a heightened sense of joy. The restored hope from Pierre was powerful and infectious. It ignited the citizens with a rippling energy. But Patricia knew from experience, that power can go both ways and so can hope.

Watching the colony's playful splashes from her dome's archway, Patricia left her home and crossed the beach to consult the only penguin who could truly assess what this meant for the colony. She arrived outside the gaping entrance and took a deep breath.

"And what you want?" an angry voice yelled from inside.

Patricia smiled, and ducked into the cave. That was as close to 'good evening' as you were going to get from Sherri.

"So busy workin' and protectin' you ain't had time for Sherri. Treating me like some old crazy in a cave. Get over here." Sherri hugged Patricia hard and quick, then pushed her away. The D.E.W.'s cave was lit with a topaz glow.

"I'm sorry Sherri. I've—"

"You ain't been nothin'."

Patricia laughed.

"What you want?" Sherri pronounced it *won't*.

"I have to ask you a question."

Patricia paused. Sherri waited. Then popped her eyes wide impatiently.

"How many eggs can this place hold?"

"We have exactly one hundred and forty six seabirds on the cape, including Pierre. Thirty families of three, forty-four couples without an egg, six widows and widowers; and six single folk. Assuming Pierre isn't spoken for."

"He isn't."

"Figured. Any bird who volunteers to watch eggs all day has a *loooong* life in front of 'em. Trust me, I know." She moved her beak, silently counting. "I can't say for sure, but we can hold a good amount. More than we have now I tell you that much."

"*How many*, if you had to guess?"

"If I had to guess, and I don't, I'd say about fifty. In any one season."

"Okay," Patricia sighed, dropping her shoulders a bit.

Sherri frowned, and inched up to Patricia's belly. "You plan on making me some eggs? You know I want them don't ya? Want 'em bad. I'm not getting any younger you know. I am not getting any younger. I am *not* getting any younger. You ain't either."

"No. No, I'm not. Thanks for your help, Sherri." Those questions and statements didn't quite hurt Patricia like they used to, but she still felt the need to flee before they started to. She knew Sherri only asked because she didn't know. Didn't know Patricia's condition.

"I'll be sure to—"

"One last thing," Sherri cut. She wasn't very loud anymore, and looked somewhat concerned. Her gaze softer. Her brow less tense. "You didn't have anything to do with that Solus Banishment, did you?"

"Banishments are the colony's choice. They happen on their own."

"Nothing happens on its own."

"Solus should have been sent away from here long before now."

"But he wasn't. Until now." There was a silence which lasted nearly three full breaths. "What did Pierre do for work when he was back home?" Sherri asked.

113

"His job. What're you getting at Sherri?"

The tiny D.E.W. circled Patricia's perfectly tall posture. "Secrets are dangerous, Patricia. We've never been a colony that keeps things from one another.

"I've always done what's best for Caterwaul."

"We all do. But nobody was calling for his departure until *you* brought it up."

"Out of fear."

"Out of wisdom. Some things are good to be left alone. Some things are good to fear. You think I got this old by being stupid? I know the fledglings here, I've raised every last one of them until they were old enough for the Academy. And I've never known one like that one you just put out. He feeds on bad circumstances. Eats hate. He needs it. He runs toward it. It makes him bigger. He's had a horrendous life. If Solus thinks you had anything to do with this—"

"*I don't care* what Solus thinks!" Patricia's sudden shout echoed within the cave. "I've handled worse."

"Okay," Sherri said, softly backing away, "Okay. Just be careful."

Patricia exited the cave. The cool night's wind rushed and blew across her face. The Caterwaul sky was a smooth obsidian with twinkles of off-white. Though Patricia tried, she couldn't spot a cloud. Patricia was always in awe at how Sherri could turn a conversation. Patricia came to see how many eggs the colony in general could raise at any one time and left thinking about her own family. Sherri was right. There had been five mating seasons since Patricia first arrived in Caterwaul. Five hopes. Five wishes. Five crushed opportunities. But, Pierre's promise changed something. Even for her. It rejuvenated her damaged optimism about the practicality and possibility of raising an egg of her own on the Cape.

Chapter 19

"There are three divisions of albatross," Aria explained, walking with Pierre along the beach the next day. "Messenger, Picker, and Courier."

The excitement from Pierre's hunting exploits the day earlier had cooled. Pierre was still grateful when Aria snuck him from the madness. Pulling him into a slim nook in the mountain as the crowd talked amongst themselves, hardly seeming to notice. Once clear, she led him in the opposite direction putting a good distance between them and the crowd. They shuffled briskly across the wet sand before slowing to stride.

Today she volunteered to enlighten Pierre about the Cape's inner workings. "Now our smallest division is the Messenger-Tross. They travel long spans through tough conditions delivering long messages. They have to battle thick rain, stinging hail, and scalding heat on almost every passing. As you can imagine, few have the stamina, strength, or memory."

"I imagine this position isn't popular," Pierre responded.

116

"Quite the opposite. Messenger-Tross is a job of great prestige. Lady birds love the Ocean Runners. Most albatross would love to be one, few have the ability."

Pierre nodded, recognizing this was some of why he wanted to become a Catcher back home. The respect of doing something admirable, without the nightmares and conflict which come with fighting in the war.

"Next, we have the Courier-Tross. Those are the ones who follow us on the hunt. They collect the fish we toss up and bring them back here to the Reserve. They have a flight system which assures there's always an albatross waiting above to intercept whatever we toss up. Yesterday, that system was broken. They'll likely have to recruit more or adjust their strategy."

Pierre wanted to apologize, but thought it a good problem to have.

"Excellent timing, swift swooping skills, and a muzzle like a trap." Aria continued. "If Messenger-Tross are our distance runners, the Couriers are the sprinters."

"How do you pick out the fast ones?" Pierre asked.

"Twelve taps of the claw is the relay time needed from the hunting area to the Reserve and back if you want to pass tryouts."

Pierre looked at the rolling ocean, imagining how far out to sea that must be from where they're standing. "And you share food?"

"Yes, they get a portion of our take."

"What if they eat the fish on their way to the Reserve?"

117

KING PENGUIN

Aria laughed and leaned forward. "We had a problem with that once. Every Catcher keeps a mental count of how many fish they collared for the trip. And for a while we couldn't figure out why the Reserve was coming up short. You can imagine who we turned to first. But we *see* all the fish Puddles eats because he does it right in front of us, so we deduct these casualties from the count."

Pierre laughed, "What did you do?"

"Well, the Sachem was furious, as always, and demanded to meet with the head of the Couriers to devise a plot to catch the thief. So, listen to this, in the middle of our hunt, we mixed in six triggerfish with what we tossed up. We gave one to each Courier. Us Catchers were trained to identify which fish were bad to eat in the Academy. But albatross and most other penguins have no clue. If eaten, a triggerfish will make you throw your guts up. Your body starts to hurt, you get dizzy, and sometimes start seeing things. When we returned from the hunt, we found an albatross and a penguin squirming in the sand, rolling around in their own fluid, shouting about dancing octopi. The two of them were working together, and were banished as the remaining triggerfish were pulled from the Reserve."

Pierre gawked, envisioning what she just said. "That's a heck of an approach."

"Don't mess with the catch. We've got a lot riding on it." She paused, then clapped. "Okay, let's see, Messenger, Courier, last

118

one is Picker. Picker-Tross search the forest for nuts, fruits, and leaves."

"Why would they do that?"

"For the Tree Dwellers who help us build. We provide the food. Mainly they want fruit and leaves but some have more exotic tastes for underwater plants like Duckweed and Hydrilla. In a situation like that, us hunters will gather it on our way back to shore."

"Tree-what?" Pierre said, overwhelmed.

"Big, hairy, and large. You'll see them sooner or later."

"I see," Pierre said, overwhelmed. "Well, that job seems pretty easy. No poisonous triggerfish, no rough weather, just gather some leaves."

She shook her head. "Common misunderstanding. Picker-Tross are the least respected birds with the most dangerous job. *They have to work the jungle.* Some have been snuck up on by a spotted leopard, others bit by a snake. Danger could be under any leaf, waiting in any tree, or behind any rock. To be an effective Picker they need piercing vision, expert knowledge of the land, and a keen investigative mind. The faster you're in and out the better. There's no time to guess. Know what you're looking for. Get it. Run."

This was all baffling. Where Pierre grew up penguins didn't work with any other animals. He had heard of something like their

Tree Dwellers in bedtime stories but they called them by a different name, and, honestly, he thought they were a myth.

"Because Pickers know their job is dangerous, but not many of us respects it as such, sometimes they tend to exaggerate the tales of their heroics. Frank, is the worst." Aria and Pierre strategically pulled alongside a huddle of albatross. The seven large white birds rustled and adjusted their feathers, before folding them neatly.

"Listen," Aria said.

Pierre leaned in. Amidst the circle of large birds, one high-pitched voice rose above the rest.

"I tell ya, there were at least ten of 'em!" the talking bird scanned the crowd, "teeth, sharp as fangs, claws, long as your head, and drooling. Drooling with a thirst for *murder*." There was some chatter as the speaking bird continued, "The hair on their fur stood up like thistles, revealing their savage nature. Then, there I was backed against a tree, tall as the sky. A thick canopy of branches overhead preventing my escape. There was nowhere to go, but straight forward," he pointed a wing, "into the belly of the beasts. A cloud slowly passed above, shining a clear ray of daylight on the far side of the hideous monsters. This was my way out. I had to get this clearing. But how? The creatures gnarled and snapped. Dry branches cracked under their heavy footsteps. Movement all around, the smaller forest residents retreated to their burrows and bushes. The monsters never even glanced at them.

That was the regular diet. They wanted something fresh. They had a taste for albatross!" he hissed, dragging the s's in 'albatross'.

"At that moment, I steadied my trembling body. I stilled my rattling nerves. To get home…I knew, I was gonna have to fight my way out."

The other birds look at one another blankly.

"Aaaaaiiiiiiiiiiyyyy chop!" The albatross continued. "I popped one on the head. *Hiiiiiiiya!* Dodged to the left. *Tah!* I jumped. *Boof!* One knocked me down. I rolled into open space, looking up. They were closing. I kicked one in the chest, so hard I heard his bones pop!" the albatross stopped, scanning the audience. "Brothers, I tell ya, it was war. Not for the faint of heart. I doubt any of you would've survived. It was just that raw!"

Aria tapped Pierre. "Frank here is referring about a pack of wild ocelots that roam the woodlands. The threat is real enough. Many birds have nearly been skinned alive by the vicious beasts which live in the forest. I never recommend going there unless you really know the lay of the land. However, do you want to know what Frank *really* came up against that day?"

Pierre slanted.

"Bunny rabbits," she said with a giggle.

"Bunny rabbits?"

"Bunny rabbits."

"How do you know?"

"Apparently, he snagged a bushel of carrots. They hopped curiously over. He vacated his stomach and ran away."

Pierre folded with laughter.

"His Co-Picker saw the whole thing," Aria continued. "Said you could follow the trail of doo all the way to the mountains!"

They were both doubled over now wheezing, trying to muzzle the sound.

"He's lying," she cackled, "and they know it."

Pierre raised his flippers. "So why listen?"

"Everyone likes to be entertained."

Aria took a while to reclaim her composure, standing up straight, exhaling with a quiver. "Woo! Ahem, but yes, that's how we coexist. Three groups, each providing services for the other in exchange for other services, or food. We do something for them, they do something for us, everyone's happy."

Pierre and Aria continued their trek, approaching the narrow, elevated entrance to Caterwaul. Pierre stopped in his tracks as his beak flew open. He looked at Aria, who was smiling. At least a dozen furry beasts descended like dinosaurs down the slope moving toward the beach. They seemed to move in slow motion. Pounding potholes into the sand. The smallest of them was at least three times Pierre's height, and the largest about five or six. Moving out of their path, Pierre stood next to his guide, awaiting instruction.

"Don't worry, they'll only eat you if you taste like a tree," she said. "They prefer plants. Not penguins."

Pierre was hoping his utter fear wasn't that obvious.

A grand mammal with burnt orange fur and a face flat as a rock passed. It stared directly down at Pierre. He swallowed. It kept a blank expression, then nodded. Pierre looked up, frozen at first, then nodded furiously not wanting to offend. Being small was new to him. So far as penguins go, King penguins were pretty tall, though he was half Gentoo, so he wasn't as tall as a pure King. But being looked down upon this sharply made him feel vulnerable and absolutely petrified.

"What are they here building today?" he asked, eyeing the giant figures tromping down the shore.

Aria shifted her focus to the twinkling objects floating on the distant sea. "Plugs."

Pierre was patient for an explanation.

Aria frowned, paused, and continued, "This place is more dangerous than most think. There's *something* out there. We're not really sure what it is. But it wasn't always there. It's getting closer. And it kills everything it touches."

Chapter 20

If Tiberius knew anyone was listening he would have kept the message to himself. Secured in the vault of his mind where it rightfully belonged. It was taught that Messengers should practice their delivery aloud. It helped ensure the proper message was delivered and in the proper tone. No bird wanted to fly across the sea, only to forget, or worse, misquote his or her message. In the emptiness of Bouvet, Messengers typically stopped for rest and repetition. Some were required to travel as far as Australia, while others flew deep into the heart of Fiji. Though Tiberius wasn't burdened with a voyage quite that far, he was the only one asked to go into an active warzone. Others risked losing their message, but for Patricia, Tiberius risked his life. The rules laid out by her and Pierre's father were always at the front of his mind, and he did his best to stay true to them.

Rule One: Enter the Falklands only at night. Well after the sun is down when the sky is darkest.

Rule Two: Know your stars. If you get lost, navigate by constellation. Everyone's heard stories of the birds that lost their way. The ocean is a desert to the inattentive, and most of the world is far less civil than home. Many lost Messengers were doomed to wander the infinite Atlantic, while others found themselves in volatile places. Cover of darkness and guidance by star were powerful allies.

Rule Three: Speak only in the old language. To protect the secrecy of the message, the Falklands relied upon their own ancient dialect, or *Viejo Lenguaje*, completely dissimilar to Caterwaul's Langue de L'ancien to spread the word. Tiberius was groomed to be fluent in both languages plus the common tongue nearly everyone spoke. Pierre's father received the message from Tiberius in Caterwaul's native *Langue* and passed it to his mother where she would relay the message in the Falklands native *Lenguaje* to his brother and other important relatives. Nothing was more precious than the message, and it could *never* be too safe.

Rule Four: Meet on high ground. Never risk ambush from above. The best advantage a bird of the sky has over one of the sea is flight. If an albatross could be pounced and weighed down, he'd be tortured for what he knows and disposed of.

Tiberius paced the glacial surface mulling over what he was to deliver. The first part: mostly Patricia responding to comments and questions from Pierre's dad in the message prior. The second: updating her brother on how Pierre was getting along. Then, a drastic change in mood as she revealed her concerns. The pit Pierre could be digging for himself, and how the Cape, for its reasons, would let him. Pierre didn't talk about it much, but she could see the deep hurt in his eyes whenever he thought he was alone. She asked her brother if things were getting better. Despite being sure they weren't, she felt it her responsibility to ask.

Tiberius rehearsed with seasoned prose. Enunciating his vowels, clicking his tongue on the hard consonants and pausing at changes in subject when he heard what sounded like claws tapping ice over his shoulder. He turned. Nothing was there. Just the loud whistle of the wind and slow lapping of the sea. Tiberius took a calm panoramic, scanning the island.

Once a Messenger was seen as careless with his cargo, he was no longer trusted. Once untrusted, no one wants to work with him. No work, no contribution. No contribution, well...

The colony learned the hard way, when one can eat and not work, others will want to know why they cannot do the same. Getting over is infectious, and sloth lay dormant in most every being. If the weed were to flourish it would consume the colony. Reeling each species back to basic levels, having to relearn how to survive on their own.

Messaging was the only thing Tiberius knew how to do. He spent his life honing the craft since Patricia drafted him. He learned repetition was the key. Preparation and practice, the two biggest factors to success and Bouvet was the only place a Courier

126

could perfect their message with complete concentration. In complete solitude alone.

Or so he thought.

Chapter 21

Solus thought the elements were playing tricks when he heard the sound of wings coming to a flutter in the distance. Solus rapped his jagged claws against the ice. Do birds come here? He always assumed it was too cold, too remote, that their feathers would freeze over if they stayed any real period of time. They simply weren't built for these arctic conditions, so why come to this place? Why would one visit here? Yet there it was. The distinctive whoosh of a bird landing and gentle pat of feet meeting the ice. The wind it created on descent was so forceful it swirled the fog for a bit. Solus admitted only one set of wings he'd had seen in all his travels were capable of whipping up such a powerful breeze.

Could it be? Solus looked down and grinned. Have our stars favored the wronged? He walked carefully toward the noise. Sneaking through the thicket of falling snow until he reached a silhouette, marvelously familiar, standing near the edge of the island. Solus didn't realize he was almost jogging until the grey shadow turned his direction. Solus quickly cut and slipped soundlessly into the sea. He moved closer through the liquid. A few feet away, his head barely above surface, Solus hid below a small shelf of ice next to Tiberius. He stayed low hearing muffled sounds distorted by the storm. Garbled statements cleared every two words, then every other word, then every word as Solus listened intently.

Chapter 22

"We first saw first symptoms in a cartographer who used to work here," Aria continued while Pierre gazed at the large ships far off shore. She pointed. "Then...dead fish, dead plants. Anything too close too lost all its color."

Pierre crumpled his brow, inspecting the details of the floating object. "Do we know what it looks like?"

"Just thick liquid, darker than the rest. Medics have been making trips to the site and returned disoriented even from the shorter trips. They found there are holes in the thing, where something black is pouring into the water. When it mixes in, the ocean becomes a smoky grey color. I don't know, but whatever is leaking from those holes, it's deadly. And we think it's spreading. It's meeting us further out. Which means it's coming closer."."

"You sure the plugs will work?" Pierre's sensed his uncertainty sounded more like pessimism.

She looked up. "I don't know. It's possible, I guess. There's speculation that if we don't obstruct the flow, Caterwaul won't last through the season."

Pierre looked out at the strange structures. He remembered the faint hum he'd heard during their expedition. It sounded low but strong, like a distant Blue Whale calling her calf to come home. But this information gave Pierre a deeper peek into the Cape. The objects on the horizon were already the second of two things Pierre had never seen before a little while ago. Pierre thought of how calm and confident Caterwaul must be to know something so lethal was coming and not be in a stupor. "If it doesn't work, what's everyone going to do?"

"Nothing," she replied too placid. "Most don't know. Just us Catchers who have to go out there, two Medics who do the inspections and the Builder working to design the plugs."

"The Cape doesn't know?"

"It's far enough off shore, and we're taking measures to stop it. What can they do, besides panic?"

"Still, shouldn't they know?"

"And take the only peace they've had since The Lack? It's taken us a long time to feel at ease again. In one day, you've given some hope. To believe they can have the family they've wanted and the life they remember. Do you want to toss that out for a hypothetical?"

Pierre's chest grew tight thinking of the dilemma. He was admittedly new. It wasn't in a place to incite a frenzy about something he just found out about plus didn't fully understand. But dark secrets had a dark past with him. When those secrets came to light, the response was nearly always dangerous.

Chapter 23

"Vous serez fier de votre fils le pingouin va devenir," Tiberius quoted, clearing his throat, adjusting his diction. *"Hier, il était nouveau et viens d'arriver. Maintenant, après une journée sur les citoyens chasse sont prêts à le traiter comme il possède l'endroit!"* The giant bird worked to deliver the passage in the same enthusiasm as Patricia. *"Ils ont mangé une fête aujourd'hui son crédit. L'Attrape-Roi est ce que certains l'appelle en privé, ne sachant pas son nom. Mais à sa vieille tante bien qu'il est tout simplement Pierre."* He paused on the part that gave him problems. *"L'Attrape-Roi. L'Attrape-Roi,"* he repeated, with varying pitch. High, then low. He paced a small section of the ice, playing with the verbiage, seeking the best approach. This was his climax. It needed to be delivered with the right energy.

He spread his wings, a massive twelve and a half feet of reddish-brown feathers, flapping every so often to keep cold pellets of snow from settling and sticking patches of them together. He tucked his wings perfectly in place and took in the island. Water, ice, mountains, and a slanting cloak of snow. Empty. Tiberius shook his neck satisfied with the solitude and, switching dialects, returned to his monologue. Reforming the phrase again and again in his speech:

"*L'Attrape-Roi. L'Attrape-Roi*," he said. "The Catcher of Kings?" No. "L'Attrape-Roi. The King's Catcher?" Doesn't make sense. "The Catcher King?" Something still doesn't translate well. What is it? He was vexed. Tiberius tried to put the words in proper context. What he knew about Pierre, about the message, about what Patricia was trying to say, about the Cape. Rays of clarity burned through a mental cloud. "The King Catcher. *L'Attrape-Roi*. Pierre, the King Catcher." Tiberius huffed his chest, impressed with his work. A good Messenger never simply regurgitates his speech like a father feeding his young. The magic was in capturing the essence of what was being delivered, and giving it in a way that made the audience feel they were there. Less theatrics. More sincerity. Less showmanship. More accuracy. Caring enough to present the message how they'd want to hear it, and always be sensitive to the unspoken truth. You are all they have. You are all that connects them.

As Tiberius primed himself for a last round before taking off, a stir swished in the liquid nearby. He turned to a sound he could only describe as unnatural. Rightfully paranoid, he etched forward fluttering his wings once more to shake loose the snow. He, then, propped them half-open readying for flight. Leaning his neck over the small edge of ice, he stared into the dark blue. What he found lit him with a strange caution. A red light gazing up from under the surface, making a rippling circular impression atop the water. What is this?

Go, Tiberius thought. Curiosity wasn't worth it. But protocol demanded he make sure the secrecy wasn't compromised. That he wasn't being spied on or careless. If the Falklands had learned of this place as a hub for the Messengers it wouldn't take long to send a scout. Information meant leverage. This was his only job, without it he'd have no contribution. For his sake, Tiberius had to be sure. The glow puzzled him as his mind raced. Maybe something was just eaten, which would explain the sound and color but not the glow?

He stretched his beak far to get a better look. His body leaning back, not to tip over. Tiberius put his ear to the water to see if he could identify the size of what he guessed an animal. If it sounded like anything bigger than a penguin he was out of here. Tiberius took shallow breaths and listened. Silence. He swiveled his head to face the water. To his horror, the fiery blaze was getting smaller at a rapid pace. More concentrated. More near. It shot into focus. *It was...a face.*

Wide jaws burst through the surface clamping Tiberius around the throat. It twisted, jerked, and snatched him asunder. Under the water, something hung heavy on his neck as Tiberius was ripped back and forth. Pain spiked in every nerve. Encased in a flurry of red bubbles, the grip tightened on his throat. Tiberius lashed wildly, hoping his talons would hit flesh. After four frantic lashes

135

his claws pushed into something plush and blubbery. The clamp around his neck quickly released. Flapping his wings trying to fly to the surface, Tiberius broke through to the world above and sucked a feast of air into his shocked lungs. Dragging onto the ice, he slid his dripping body across the cold frigid ground, pushing away from the edge. He staggered to his feet still gasping. Stepping backwards, his gaze locked on the ocean, he flapped his wings but the salty liquid was soaked to the bone. He jumped to takeoff and plummeted down with a damp hard smack. His clumped feathers felt heavy as rock. He tried again, this time managing to hover a foot or two before falling back to Earth. He shook, rigorously flinging beads of water. Tiberius felt horrified he couldn't maintain flight. Dropping into the ocean wounded prey would leave him worse than staying on land. If he didn't shed the water in his wings before it iced he'd never leave alive.

A shiny plateau about six feet high was in the distance. Tiberius needed to get to that perch. He needed a safe place to dry. He needed to see what was coming. Turning and running, he heard a loud splash. Tiberius looked back to see a black and white blur torpedo from of the ocean with such force it looked like the Atlantic spit him out. Sliding on a slick stretch of ice, it rose, tall and scarred. Tiberius knew this bird. He took a step back, then another and another. He thought for sure he'd seen him for the last time. Yet, standing in front of him, glistening in the glum grey was the outcast. The one he'd watched carried out of Caterwaul without a thought. Ooze trickled from three fresh puncture wounds on Solus' left chest from Tiberius' attack.

Just a few yards between them Tiberius' glare trailed up to the crimson pockets of light burrowed in Solus' head. The snow fell diagonally in a steady flush and Solus looked in no rush to pursue. The albatross grew more alarmed. He couldn't fly and his adversary was counting on it. The drip of Tiberius' feathers kept him surrounded in a shallow pool of water.

Snnnap! Snnnap! Echoes shot through the vacant landscape. The clap of Solus' beak sounded like a thick branch breaking and after a sudden shudder, Tiberius slipped. Fumbling and wet, struggling to stand with his webbed feet quickly slipping from under him, Tiberius could feel something climbing inside of him. Something he had only heard of. Something he never felt. Immediate fear. Not the fear that comes with going in and out of the Falklands. A fear which became more diluted with each safe passage. This was present, material, dark, mounting, and specific.

Tiberius kicked his trembling feet, the efforts doing little to move him along the ice. His short talons slipping, scratching, and scraping.

Tiberius discovered the 'who' but struggled with 'why.' Tiberius couldn't bring Solus back. So, why had *he* been dragged under the cold stinging sea? Why was he badly bruised and standing on a deserted island with Solus? Why was Solus doing this? Tiberius hoped Solus didn't remember him watching at his

Banishment. The thought raced and the bird couldn't locate bravery. Solus was here because they put him here. Specifics meant less to Solus than it did to him. Solus was marooned, convinced of a notion which festered in his mind. And today, Tiberius represented an entire Cape. Tiberius huffed, bracing as Solus reached the base of his frame.

Chapter 24

Solus inched closer toward the cowering albatross. Gazing down upon him, Solus basked in his victories. What he did to Paul. The wonderful rumble of the professor's home crashing in the distance. The quake it sent rolling across the island. Something that badly damaged was destined to break. He would join Flora after all. Solus shoveled the thought from his mind with a grin, focusing on the now. The ever-so-noble albatross was in his presence, and deserved his full attention. After all, it was time for the extraction. Paul, in a stuttering panic forfeited half a treasure, and the rest was sunken inside this messenger.

The island's already dismal visibility was worsening through the shield of falling snow. Earlier, Solus could only see eight or nine steps in front of him. Now, that eight or nine had easily dropped to five. The riot of white was blinding, racing like chariots to the ground, and Solus kept close proximity to his prisoner. Creeping forward as Tiberius slid, weighted to the cold ice trying to push back on a wet webbed foot.

Tiberius swung. He swung again. The heavy wet wing arched in slow motion as Solus calmly leaned back once, then again.

Rolling over, hopping to his feet, Tiberius fluttered, managing to hover three feet. He lunged at Solus with his golden beak. The penguin dropped one foot back and turned sideways. Tiberius zipped past, turned and slid to a stop. Solus charged. Clapping his wings in front of him, sending a powerful burst of wind into Solus' chest. The wings were no good for flying, but they still commanded enough force to drive Solus back on the slick surface.

Solus squinted, struggling through the onslaught, watching water flick from the bird's feathers with every thrust. Solus growled, anchoring his claws into the ice, clamoring forward. Tiberius flapped harder, in strong wide strokes. Solus pressed, steadily putting one foot in front the other and the gap was shriveling, as the wind-punch seemed to beat harder. Solus was pushed through, nearly touching the tip of Tiberius' feather. Tiberius shifted his wings, dropping them for flight. Solus shot forward without the added resistance.

Tiberius lifted. Four quick kicks and Solus dropped flat on his stomach. The sound of his body rushing across the ice was like running water. Tiberius shakily tilted and leaning left to right, climbing, drifting further from Bouvet. Solus clenched tighter. Tiberius leveled himself, giving a hard push. Solus popped to his feet and leapt.

A cloud seemed to pass as unobstructed sunlight shot through with the snow. Solus found a hard knob of bone in his beak, and with a whipping turn, Solus swung Tiberius' body to the hard surface, slamming with a loud crack.

The albatross cringed, shrieked, yelled, rolled over, and kicked. Solus impatiently swatted away the kicks. Standing over Tiberius' body, Solus hammered his ribcage with his thick flipper until he heard something split. Tiberius' body went limp. Only a shallow breath lightly moved the shell. Tiberius winced, curling into a ball before Solus slid his foot up the bird's neck pinning him flat to the cold hard ice.

"I'm no fool," Solus said, panting softly "I know exactly how this works. For one to come, one must go. Only room for so many stomachs. I was the chosen sacrifice, but I should have been immune. After all, how could Caterwaul survive without its greatest Catcher? How could it get along without, me and the beak that feeds it? In my position, I've had time to think and it didn't take long to see. There was one way. You found yourself a replacement. An upgrade, so you think. Someone who could do my job, who could carry my load without disappearing, someone you thought was consistent and at that point I became expendable. Something to be cast out and driven into the wild. Pierre...the King Catcher!" he said with sarcastic regality. "As you so lovingly call him. Summoned from some place called the Falklands so you could get rid of me. Ouch. That hurt. But you're in the business of telling things, so tell me something." Solus leaned down, whispering, "How can I meet him?"

Tiberius held silent. Solus straightened his slouched frame, tilting his head backwards before rolling it around in a full circle and whipping it back down.

"There are two options," Solus said. "And I think you're smart enough to assume what they are." Solus slid his foot further up Tiberius' neck. The albatross squirmed, twisting for an inch as Solus jammed his outside claws into the ice on both the sides creating a jagged barricade around the messenger's throat.

"Wiggling would be ill-advised. Tell me what I want to know and don't you lie like my mother."

Solus slowly descended his middle talon, sifting through a thin layer of feathers, and prickling against bare skin. Solus wanted the him to know the price of refusal. Tiberius short shallow breaths. Solus, pressed his nail harder with every breath. Tiberius' eyes grew wide with the steady rush of snow falling at his sides. The skin felt thin. One more breath and it would give.

Chapter 25

It didn't take an experienced builder to see the dome was on its last limb. The master mold for Caterwaul's dome, once perfectly arched, was bent lopsided and slumped when a gentle breeze galloped through the fog and pushed a loose block to the inside. The house went down with a thunder. But he wasn't in it. He left Flora and he wasn't proud of it. Had he been within they would've shared the same fate. Staring at the rubble, Paul was compelled to weep, but couldn't. History wouldn't repeat itself. He'd cried that cry. Seasons ago and many since. Paul looked up into the snowy overcast imagining Pyxis would soon be twinkling bright. His chest rose and sunk inhaling the strange flower-scented air which occasionally visited the tundra. Paul grew warm.

He basked. But soon his brief smile slipped into a concerned glare. He gave Solus a name. He didn't mean to. He didn't wish to. But that didn't change things. By whispering Pierre's name, he put him in the path of a powerful danger. Solus had made Paul panic.

The panic flurried his thoughts. Thoughts became mumbles. Mumbles became barely audible words. Then it was over.

Paul felt a lump of shame. Shame in how he behaved. Shame in what he temporarily wanted. Shame in what, in that moment, he didn't want anymore. The Celestial Nest, though a destination, should never grow become a desire. Paul realized in that moment, when his house was crumbling, that his yearning for the life after was a temporary thirst. Losing Flora dug a deep pit. Sadness tossed in his mind and sank in his heart until he believed there was nothing left. His thoughts were the easiest way to deal with a life which had long since become too hard to live. Yet, when faced with the escape he wanted, a free ride, a blind ferryman who requested no token, Paul couldn't get on the boat.

There was something he had to do now. A difficult purpose. Pierre would suffer a worse fate at Solus' mercy than that of any leopard seal, because Paul knew the most vicious predators of all are your own kind. Paul, once again, found himself tasked to save a King. Searching east down the island, he found a trail of webbed footprints filling quickly with the falling snow. Paul lowered his head and entered the storm.

Walking cautiously, he pursued who he thought to be Solus. The worsening grey overcast made it impossible to tell how long he had been on the hunt. Shrouded by snowstorm, Paul followed tracks and responded to noise. At times, Paul heard shuffling nearby and stopped. Other times, he heard faint rustlings afar and

144

rushed to them, quietly, like quick whispers, closing the distance. Fits of nervousness tempted Paul to attack whenever he thought Solus to be near and be done with it. Yet somehow, such actions he thought would serve the dual function committing suicide and accomplishing nothing. He couldn't do both. And at this point, he decided he wanted neither. What the old professor really desired and needed was the plan brewing to remove Pierre. Paul felt adrenaline tingle his body hearing the splutter of spiteful thoughts echo from a voice undoubtedly Solus'. Paul kept sly attention, analyzing best he could the thoughts of a predator.

Snow seemed to cover the footprints faster and Paul had to shrink the distance not to lose track. Dropping too far behind would assure he'd get lost. Closer and closer Paul could hear the Fiordland's steps crush soft ground. Paul stopped. Exhaling with a quiver he stepped, lightly as his body allowed. His heart thumped in palpitations as the prints cut off at the water's edge. Paul doubled over, pondering if Solus had just left Bouvet with Pierre's name. If he had gone back to Caterwaul like an angry pup pushing for an udder when there isn't enough milk? Looking to be loved by someone with none to spare. Maybe Caterwaul was the only thing that ever loved him. No matter how brief or circumstantial. For his abilities, whether they liked it or not, he was loved. Now, without that purpose, Solus was exactly what life always told him he was. Worthless. Abandoned by a father and the least concern of a mother, who focused more on her mate who wasn't there than the fledgling who was. And now, cast from his only home to make room for a better offspring. A nobler son.

Standing at its edge, the ocean slapped against the island. Paul gazed across the grayish waves. Going in would put him at a disadvantage, even more than on land. He turned and looked into the slanting snow. Solus' footsteps or grumbles could no longer be heard. Yet, despite limitless possibilities of travel, and how bad Solus wanted to return home, his primal strength was no match for a swarm of Preservers. Everyone knew his name. Everyone knew his face. There was no sandy expanse, no corner, crevice, or crèche for him to hide in or live amongst.

A crack, like the loud split of ice, echoed in the mist. Paul rushed to the sound. Through a haze, he saw something misshapen. One body, no, two. Solus was standing, but something was under him. Approaching the brink of his cover, Paul saw a large bird pressed tightly under Solus' foot. Paul steadied to charge. He drew a deep breath. Focusing on Solus, bits of the conversation unclenched Paul's muscles. Something was off. There was no struggle from the prey, no cry, no fight. Were they enemies? How could he be sure? If he rushed into this conversation would it be two-on-one in his favor? The pinned bird sounded calm, like water in a brook. Certainly, more relaxed than Paul earlier that afternoon at Solus' mercy. Something *was* wrong.

146

KING PENGUIN

Bouvet's howling wind made it impossible to take in every word. As Paul slid his foot forward, the head of the albatross turned sharply his direction.

Chapter 26

Solus' victim remained silent. Despite the façade, Solus saw a deepening fear seeping from every unchecked motion. Every dash of the eye. Each shift of the torso. Every tremble, every quickened breath and swallow betrayed the albatross' cool exterior. Yet, the bird seemed determined to resist.

"Secrecy," Solus muttered. "A decree from penguins which is more important than your own life. Tell me something Tiberius, do you even know what you'd be dying for?"

Tiberius met Solus' gaze.

"A rule you have no say in making, but must follow even unto death." Solus leaned down, widening his eyes. "Does that make you equal? Does that make you a partner? Would *they* die for *your* secrets?"

"I swore an oath," the albatross gritted, slightly stretching his neck.

"You yielded to obligation and mistook it for choice?" Solus pressed harder upon Tiberius' throat. "You're a tool. And if you break, you'll be replaced."

"I'm not."

Solus cocked his head, a sly grin smeared across his face. "You think you're free?"

"I am free."

"Because you get to pick your own fish from the pile? You have wings to see the world. And only go where they tell you."

"That was my choice." Tiberius squirmed against the ice. "I chose to be a Messenger."

"Having an option isn't the same as having a choice. You had to be something. Had to fit into a pre-ordained hole. What would you be if you had your say? If you didn't need them for a place to eat and a safe place to sleep? Would your entire life still be flying chatter between distant penguins?" Solus scoffed. "That's what genuine freedom is. Creating your own journey. Not picking from a list."

"*I'm free,*" Tiberius winced.

"You desire to be good. You think you need her approval. That's why you deny me. Well, here's your approval; would *Patricia* want you to tell a secret and live, or keep it and die here in the middle of nowhere?" Solus' eyes scanned his victim. "All I want is information."

Tiberius' gaze fell, then looked to the left. He turned his head, dragging Solus' talon half the width his throat. It scraped the surface of Tiberius' pink skin. A thin stream of blood dripped onto the ice.

"Decision time."

Solus took a deep breath and pushed his foot deeper into the bird's neck. A swell of air caught at the base of Tiberius' throat. Red claws stretched from the corners of Tiberius' sclera. He flinched. He squinted. He fought to move. He shut his eyes tight as if trying to wish it away. Then, he opened them again. Finally, Tiberius looked at Solus and parted his beak.

Chapter 27

Behind the wall of fog, Paul Jaunty heard the words he didn't wish to hear. Frozen to his core, he realized he could no longer stay in hiding. He wiggled his flippers, took two quick breaths and charged from the thicket of blinding white wall of snow. Taking Solus by surprise, Paul shouldered Solus square in the stomach, sending him into the thick cover of fog and snow.

"What did you tell him?" Paul barked to the albatross lying on the ice, keeping his vision trained to where Solus disappeared.

"*What* did you tell—" Paul glanced down. He had to do a double-take. Tiberius was in total shock.

Paul feared the worst, nudging Patricia's Trans-Atlantic to his feet. A trail of dark blood now crawled down the albatross' radiant white breastplate. The albatross looked at Paul, then searched the ground. Paul squinted and clenched his jaw. Ultimately, he too gave Solus what he sought. A piece to the puzzle. His gaze grew soft. He was just as mad with himself. Who knew what Solus would do once he had all the pieces he needed.

"Can you fly?" Paul shouted. His focus dashed between the wounded albatross and the blinding curtain of snow.

The albatross crooked his wings to full-span.

"Try! Go! Tell Patricia Pierre's in danger! She'll know what to do. Tell her Solus is coming!"

Tiberius was a statue.

"Albatross! Look! Nothing's happened yet. We can stop this. We can still fix it. But we have to fix it now. Right now. So, get the flip out of here!"

Tiberius crouched then exploded wildly into the falling snow. His wings throbbed as he raced through the storm. He looked down through the flurry. Solus and Paul were locked in a vicious struggle. Sharp pain ran from the middle of his chest the tip of wings causing him to dip and lull, being tossed around by the angry wind. He wondered if he could complete the short trip. Or, would fall into the Atlantic, a wet, wounded treat for anything with teeth. Leaving the island which should've been his grave, Tiberius felt guilt like a boulder deep in his gut. For not just his words, but his thoughts. A virus was spreading in his mind and he couldn't shift his thoughts from one simple theme: *Am I free?*

Chapter 28

Paul scurried, pressing deeper into the snow and fog with Solus in hot pursuit. Flashes of red flickered from his radiant eyes in the white snowfall every time Paul looked back. Stinging cuts from burned along the length of Paul's side from their struggle. Paul needed to get out of here. Once the storm passed, which he knew could be any moment, he would lose his cover. Coming to the edge of the water, Paul gently eased himself in. The blood from his wounds seeped like tree branches into the greyish ocean. He swam softly along the ice's edge, sensing Solus was close. Something stirred in the water below. Paul stopped his movement. He could hear Solus breathing. Heavy. Deliberate. Taunting. A red glow swept the area and Paul lowered himself to be even with the ice, leaving only head and eyes exposed.

"Come out and I will end this for you. No more misery. No more being afraid. How warm would it be? To finally have real peace. I can help. I will help." Paul heard a clicking every few words, as Solus' hard, overgrown talons tapped ice. "It's time to get what you deserve. Lay down your burden. And let me give you rest."

The red light sweeping the haze suddenly vanished. Paul gaze raced back and forth across the fog. Stuck between Solus' vengeance and a vicious ocean which had already picked up the scent of blood, swimming to the nearest island was sheer suicide. There were no good options left. Fight one predator or several? No escape. One of them had to go. Paul grimaced. And slowly slid out onto the ice.

Chapter 29

Fifty cycles of the sun had now passed and Pierre gazed upon Caterwaul's many new faces with concern. It was now deep into the mating season and the colony was taking full advantage of his accidental oath. Moreover, in little more than seven weeks his position within the Cape was changing. He saw it. He felt it. Citizens staring while he wasn't looking, using titles instead of his name, apologizing for absolutely nothing. He feared becoming less perishable, less of a penguin, less real. Their noble regard somehow felt belittling, like the praise was turning him into stone. Someone to hypothesize about, its thoughts its ways, rather than a penguin you can study and witness. Perhaps it really is more fun to wonder. He himself knew up close, where he grew up was a war-torn, food-deprived wasteland, but from afar he wondered. Wondered what his family was doing, what they talked about at the end of the day, what thing could still make them laugh.

Wee-Waddlers, Tee-Waddlers, and even some elders spent their lunch on the shore guessing how many he would collar. Three small penguins escalating in height kept a designated position, where their conversations repeated without waver.

"How many do you think he'll catch today?" one would typically say.

"If I had to guess, seven-hundred. You?" responded the other.

"Seven-fifty."

Then, they'd both turn to the smallest one. "And what about you, Bella?"

A fairy penguin with soggy cheeks and bright blue eyes looked up. "Four," she said, absolutely sure, before tending to her mound of sand.

They exchanged predictions, and without fail, the total wouldn't disappoint.

Yet, life wasn't giving what he asked for. When Pierre thought on it, he wanted: safety, family, fun. It was warming to know while stuck here, he could offer aid. But their pouring admiration, while appreciated, often felt misplaced. The sheer number of fish here made them very easy to catch. Pierre was accustomed to hunting in a vast overfished part of the sea where game was scarce. He exhausted often himself to return to the shore with only a few fish. His success wasn't part of a special knack he hatched with, but a sad factor of what he had to do to survive. He wanted no glory, no homage, no privileges. Yet, fending hubris became increasingly difficult. Oh, how it felt to be good at something.

KING PENGUIN

Pierre was never special or important to anyone who wasn't blood-related. But, for now, marooned on this isle of sand, he truly felt a King. He walked straighter, kept better eye-contact, spoke clearer. Preservers showed him private trails to secret parts of the Cape. He was constantly asked to skip the line at the Reserve. The Builders fashioned for him a lavish residence four times the size of any other. He can only remember sleeping in it a handful of times to show his respects, but preferring to stay with his aunt and uncle. Perhaps it was innocence, or kindness, or sheer persuasion but either way it made living in this limbo a little better.

After another exhausting day, Pierre settled in the comfort of his favorite lookout. A high hill where he came to watch the Cape play. Every day after the work was done the penguins gathered together to relax and play at sea. Pierre admired their community. He gazed over splashes in the sunset and exhaled to sleep.

Chapter 30

Pierre woke to the sound of someone gasping for air. He quickly sprung up to a vision of Aria breathing heavily with her back to him looking out at the view. Pierre wasn't sure why she paid him a visit but while she sought to catch her breath he had a nagging question. A critical gap in his Caterwaul history which he needed filled.

"Can I ask you something?" Pierre asked.

Aria straightened, chasing her breath. "You just did."

They both snickered, mocking the Sachem. One of the Catchers *asked to ask* something every day just to hear his recycled wit.

Aria and Pierre's laughter fell into a giggle before Pierre continued, "It didn't seem right to ask in a crowd. And somehow we always seem to be in one. But, what is The Lack?"

Pierre heard the phrase whispered in huddles. A certain reverence accompanied the words, but over time, he heard it less and less. She hung her head. Then turned around. Her eyes found his.

"I'm sorry, I..." Pierre stood to his feet.

She took another breath and walked to the edge. "You've earned the right to know. You should know. I'm sorry I didn't tell you sooner. Not too long ago, we had a really rough time here. There was a famine. So to speak. The fish were there, but we couldn't harness enough to feed the growing number of beaks. We started taking turns, half of the citizens ate every other sunset to make sure there was enough. That turned into every two sunsets, then three. Soon, chaos erupted as penguins stormed the Reserve, taking what they could for themselves and their family. More Preservers were charged with governing the rations. Which led to fewer predator scouts, and a drop in civil policing. This Cape buckled into anarchy. Many died of starvation or left. Some were stealthily robbed of their supply. Others were beaten in the night for what they had."

Pierre crept up next to her near the edge of the hill.

"Worst part, we couldn't do anything. There was no way to fix it. It's scary when you're doing everything and it's just not enough. Which, is why I'm here. The Cape is getting bigger Pierre. And I know you won't be here forever." She paused, her gaze fell to the floor. "If we could barely support the citizens we had when you arrived, what are we going to do with this group twice its size once you leave?" Aria peered down at the citizens at play. "We're not prepared for this."

Aria turned to Pierre. "They think you'll be here forever. I've accepted that you won't. If this is still the dilemma come your departure, it'll be The Lack all over again."

Pierre followed the logic, but still felt something stir.

"Aria, if I get a chance to go home, I'm going to take it."

"I know. I would never ask you not to. But, it's bigger than that. You won't live forever. Everyone down there is too blissful and blind to realize what I did the other day. No matter how or when, we *will* be without Pierre Oiseau one day, and there is nothing I can do to stop it."

Pierre thought to rebut and counter her position, but couldn't find the words. He never pondered life after his own. And before Aria threw it in his face like Paul Jaunty's Chub, he never had to.

"Our system is flawed," she continued. "We can't rest our future on the slim shoulders of some penguin passing in the night."

"Hey, they're not that slim," Pierre grumbled, double checking.

"I'm serious. We need more. We need a plan. Either way you look at it, sir, you're not enough."

Pierre looked out over the citizens, peering down upon them from his secluded sandy hill. He tried to count the bunch, but lost his count. Pierre turned to Aria.

"What should we do?"

Chapter 31

Pierre's father used to tell him fair is a word used for weather. That adults dealt in reality, which rarely ever is. Aria was bold and presumptuous, commanding Pierre take responsibility for their future, when all he's tried to do was help since he was essentially banished here. After their talk, one stubborn theme hung in his mind: I don't belong to them. I am not theirs to delegate. Why is this mine to fix? He asked again and again. But in the silence of his reflection, he knew he was only complaining. In this reality, which wasn't fair, there was no room for righteous reasoning. The truth was frightening. Tiny new faces sprinkled the shore, hard to ignore and even harder to keep track of. A faithful bunch was always there whenever he came striding out of the frothy Atlantic to greet him with an onslaught of questions. The Cape wasn't at capacity anymore, it was above it. Despite stretches of open real estate, Pierre wondered if and how badly the colony had bred beyond its means.

KING PENGUIN

When he came to Caterwaul and realized he had a positive skill, Pierre just wanted to do what he thought he could. Contribute to their system and help rebuild some of what was lost. He didn't care about the numbers of beaks to feed. If everyone was full, then the Catchers did their part. But Aria made him realize the system they created was unsustainable. And what would come of it once he was removed was...the thought shook him.

Convinced, Pierre worked twice a day with the crew of Catchers after every expedition to sharpen their hunting skills. Brainstorming with Aria and the Sachem, they came to a mixture of what the seasoned locals honed at home and the immigrant King penguin developed on faraway islands. The result was called the Amalgam. A six-point regiment to boost every critical skill necessary in hunting.

Number One: Weight Resistance. Small rocks were wrapped to the penguin with kelp as it swam distance. The added bulk and forced change of direction were designed to enhance strength of each stroke. Common knowledge said a penguin could get to the hunting zone in roughly two hundred taps of the claw. Their initial goal was one hundred and ten. Fatigue was a major factor which accounted for drop in production on the third and fourth rounds of the hunt. They had to be more effective for longer. Stamina and power were the root.

Number Two: Blind-Catch. Lead a Catcher out to a fruitful part of the sea. Then spin him or her a dozen times. The disorienting

162

effect disrupted their sense of direction. The Catcher had to decipher real prey from their mind's hazy projections quickly before their dinner got away. Hunting while dizzy served to optimize focus, and heighten reliance on other senses. As the fish move in the water around you, you feel it ripple against your feather and wave over your body. Through sensation you can sometimes see better than with your eyes. Many of the Catcher's chased blurry hallucinations through the deep dark blue, thinking they'd gotten their prey. Only to snap down and have the prey dissipate. *Vision can be the crutch.* Sometimes you have to feel your way through.

Number Three: Lasso Sync. Timing is everything. Especially in a group. Assuring the Wranglers were at equal distance and equal speed when circling fish was paramount. For Stragglers to make the most out of that brief, panicked explosion of fish, they had to be able to time exactly when it was going to occur. When left guessing, their reactions were too early or too late. Letting precious catch swim away. The team practiced their lasso relentlessly, making sure they were meticulously in tune with one another. As a more functional unit they could catch more fish with less energy.

Number Four: Agility Trials. The coral reef extending out from the Cape Caterwaul was a beautiful maze of pockets, tunnels, and bends, providing an ideal obstacle course for reactionary and agility training. They'll never try to outswim you in a straight line.

For small fish, even their base instinct quickly tells them that isn't going to work. Instead, they make lightning quick cuts. Frantic and irrational, hoping to do with agility what they could not do with speed. The group wove through colorful craters, rolling, dropping, and sprinting through gaps in the living reef. Their prey had no preconceived plan, pattern or process. Which made agility all the more valuable.

Number Five: Chase and Escape. You won't always be the only one looking for a meal. In the event you find yourself on the fish's end of the bargain, you'll want to know what to do. The Sachem orchestrated simulated chases, issued at random every day catches with the help of some Preservers. Some days, even he didn't know when they were going to ambush. A real enemy has no schedule. Thus, Sachem and Pierre thought it best they be as prepared as the crew. The exercise was designed for one thing—practicing calculated responses despite the surge of adrenaline. Pierre reminded the group that if you have to choose between life and the Catch, choose the former. This theme was difficult for Aria once she was locked in on a catch.

The last provision was something Pierre individually requested. Pierre still thought it unsafe that citizens outside their privileged circle had no clue of the danger posed by those monsters sitting far out on top the ocean. Yet, spreading hearsay and inciting a State of Emergency wasn't really his call to make.

However, with Catchers going out there every day they at least should be able to identify what the danger looked like. Sick hunters helped no one. Dead ones even less. The areas saturated with the grey underwater clouds Pierre saw on his first expedition became known as The Still since everything within their clouds was withered and motionless. Plants lost their vibrant green color, stationery sea life suffered a worse fate. The coral in those sections were brittle, ash-white stretches of skeleton. It was a graveyard and nothing was exempt if it stayed in those poisonous pockets. Medics noted the darkness of the toxin had been steady since the plugs were applied which was good news, since there was no significant change since the day Pierre met the Tree Dwellers. A secret triumph for the eight penguins in the know – three Catchers, two Builders, two Medics, and Patricia.

As the days rolled by, marching toward the mating season, Pierre reminded the group to focus on what they could control. He reminded them that the progress being made was very exciting, and one day, they'd be better than him. The truth was far less hopeful. Pierre had schemed and thought, planned and plotted, prepared, collaborated, tinkered, and taught. Came early, stayed late, and gave individual sessions but the awkward reality came piercing through in words mumbled by the Sachem in passing by one tired afternoon.

"I guess you can't teach talent. We all have our gifts. And our burdens. Sometimes they're the same. I don't know. Heck, I'm exhausted," he said, trucking toward his dome.

It was no secret Pierre had come from another place. A different hunting ground. In the season since he arrived he'd been asked more times about his catching than he'd been asked his first name. Citizens more concerned with what he was and what he could offer rather than who. How could he blame them? Pierre Oiseau didn't matter nearly as much as 'The King Catcher.' They said it with reverence. It made him uneasy that they felt he was their gift. Their retribution from the stars for taking so many of their penguins some time ago. The Lack, being their ebb and Pierre, their flow. It was scary.

Fortunately, the Sachem had it wrong on one account. It wasn't talent. Pierre was considered an average Catcher at best back home. It was evolution. Pierre wasn't better by just skill or repetition. As the scarce prey evolved to avoid being caught, the Falklands race of penguins evolved to catch them. Here there was no risk. No lack of nearby food. No direct consequence for failure. Here, they wouldn't starve for lack of fish but rather their inability to catch it. If they didn't get all they needed the first go round, they'd simply go out and try again. And again, and again, until exhaustion. But when you have only one chance to get it right. When you've seen completely empty ocean in every direction, and may come across five fish in a day, every attempt had to be your absolute best. When you're absolutely starving, you catch with the fuel of desperation. That was the instinct Pierre couldn't turn off. The motor hardwired to his aggression. He still hunted every time like it was his last and only chance. How can you simulate that? How can you manufacture life and death when the subject knows at some level it's not real, and thus is still holding back a piece of their full potential?

The Catchers worked tirelessly. They were no doubt getting better. Stronger swimmers, an improved tactical team, extended endurance, but their free flow instincts, accuracy of senses, and reactions in the moment paled in comparison to where they needed to be. Harsh as it was, there was no prize simply for effort. No one can live on that. They had to meet the call. As time wore on he saw his failure day in, day out. Having to approach it with a false, encouraging smile hurt more.

Watching the crew go sun up to sundown fed a digging depression. The population was on the run, growing rapidly just within the last few weeks. The line at the Reserve stretched along the beach. The evening swim became incomprehensibly massive. Pierre swore he saw ten new penguins a day. The youth spoke as if his title was their first words, jawing the three syllables, raising a pointed flipper, wide-eyed and off-balance, still inexperienced with their new bodies. Standing in front of the Reserve, Pierre looked at the diminished collection of food for the day. He plucked out the last one, and scooped it over to a fluffy grey fledgling staring at him shamelessly. As Pierre stood watching her trip thrice in five steps, he leaned against the depleted Reserve. His gaze hung listlessly, beginning to realize the sad and smothering truth.

He was trapped.

Chapter 32

Stopping short of the faded silver dome, Patricia centered herself for the worst. Despite her tender emotions, she had to be his rock. For Tiberius, flying was his life, his badge of pride, and for him to be grounded hurt her almost as much as him. Stepping inside, the sand looked like tiny frozen waves colored in tan. Everything within this dome was heard with disturbing definition, as her footsteps crunched the soft sand. Tiberius laid on a bed of large ovular dark green leaves across the circular room. His neck slowly turned and his small black eyes watched Patricia approach.

"Nice twirl, but you could've stuck the landing," Patricia said, stopping a few steps short.

Tiberius grunted and made a difficult roll onto his side. The smooth, round rocks of his bed clicked against one another as he moved.

"The Medics said you told them you hit a storm and were thrown down on Bouvet. Others say you said you were attacked on the Falklands. Do you remember what happened?"

"It's all a bit blurry."

"How do you feel now?"

His gaze fell to the floor.

"We don't have to discuss it. I'm just glad you're in good condition."

He nodded. Then, there was silence.

"Okay, well, they said I should let you rest. So." She leaned over and patted him on the head. "I'll visit again tomorrow." She turned for the opening.

"Patricia," Tiberius asked, sounding concerned. "I can leave, right?"

His words hung in the empty space. Patricia pivoted. "What do you mean?"

"I mean, if I wanted to leave, I could."

"You could. But those wings will take time. Besides how would you eat? Where would you sleep? It's not safe outside here."

"The Falklands aren't safe, you let me fly there."

"Because I trust my brother would let nothing happen to you."

He swallowed, rolling onto his back. "What happens if I can't run errands anymore? What becomes of me?" Tiberius was looking up at the ceiling.

"We'll have to wait and see."

"What do you *think* will happen?"

"I don't know," she said with a drop in her voice. "I don't know."

Tiberius closed his eyes, and slowly rolled to face the wall.

Chapter 33

Whenever he closed his eyes Tiberius saw himself falling from a gold-plated sky. Flailing. Yelling. Crashing into rough sand. A small gawking party on the shore standing like tiny black spots watched him plummet. The vision stopped with the small explosion of specks. A flash of red. Then black. Before being moved by a troop of Medics pushing their way through a condensed crowd. The Medics paused and Tiberius looked down at his bent, twisted wings. Then, the ground seemed to quake as a tall furry giant parted the crowd. It blocked the sun, then reached down and grabbed him.

The next morning when Tiberius woke he was mummified in kelp. His quarters in the Wellness Ward were an arched bastille. He hated every pale grey surface, each side resembling the other. He missed the caw of gulls, the chatter of penguins, the rolling smash of open sea. This place was an eerie asylum.

There wasn't any work for him since Patricia placed his runs on hold. She visited every morning, carrying in her mouth a rare fish for him to try. Or some novelties she found patrolling the island. She was his only tie to the outside world and the time between her visits drove him stir-crazy. He was accustomed to being busy. Being active. Being of use. Having missions and distractions, but in the silence, there was only time to think. Think about the episode with Solus. Their conversation. His future.

He had forty-nine nights of recovery with necessary daily care before he *should* be able to fly again. *Should* was the word he could've done without. If they were wrong, he had nothing to contribute. Nothing to offer. Of what use is a wounded, grounded albatross? How long before the pity waned and they started to call for his Banishment too? What could Patricia, well intentioned as she may be, really do to hold them off? What would she do? Tiberius was breathing deeply. His chest swelling and caving.

It saddened him to think of Caterwaul citizens as *them*, but he remembered with great accuracy how things were before. Before they found out he had something to give. Before he had purpose. He remembered what *they* were prepared to do. He didn't want to betray Patricia, but he also didn't want to go back. He couldn't. He was a parentless albatross who didn't know how to fish. His choices felt restricted. He was running out of time. Being on the wrong side of this transition, this potential transfer of power, when it came to pass meant life or death. Tiberius lay there, staring up at the curved ceiling of the off-white dome. He sighed. Solus made an offer. Tiberius had to make the best decision.

Chapter 34

Tiberius' current condition impacted Pierre deeply. The reports provided by the albatross were the only news Pierre had of home. The once impeccable bird, with blinding white perfectly aligned feathers, was now damaged and discolored. Wraps of seaweed covered his chest and stained his feathers with tinges of dark green. This dark green mixed with the dark red of his dried blood from the attack. Pierre barely recognized Patricia's confidant as he eased up next to him at the Reserve.

"This isn't fair," Tiberius said, his typically booming voice now sounding shriveled and faint.

"I'm sorry for what happened," Pierre replied.

"Not this," Tiberius snipped. He waved a bent, seaweed wrapped wing across his wounds. "This is collateral. This is my service. My obligation. What's unfair is how any of us would have to be in a place against our will."

"Sometimes we can't change our situations."

"I believed that once. But I've come to learn power comes in taking steps. Doing what you have to, even when it's uncomfortable."

Pierre frowned. "What do you mean?"

"I've seen your parents. Talked to them. They miss you very much." Tiberius touched Pierre's shoulder. "The same expression they usually have, I see on you. This was never meant to be permanent, Pierre. This was a temporary thing, one day ending in you leaving this place forever. But maybe for that to happen you'll have to play a part."

"How?"

"Has anyone ever told you about the Great Excavation?"

Pierre shook his head.

Tiberius sneered, rolling his eyes. "Typical. It's an event, at the end of every mating season."

"What happens?"

"I've never been. I'm told it's a celebration. Seabirds from every island anywhere come to share in knowledge, food, and games. A place, usually meant for fun, but in your case…"

"You think someone may know something about the Falklands? About the war?"

Tiberius shrugged. "Who knows? These penguins come from all over. Everywhere! What would be your loss?"

Pierre felt like he was grasping at frail hope. But with the Messenger grounded what other option did he have? At this point, he didn't even know if his parents were doing well. Or even still alive.

The albatross raised a brow. "If you don't go how can you know? I'm no use to you in this condition, and likely may never be any use to you again."

Pierre was unaware the damage was so extensive. "Don't say that."

"Just being honest. And no one else is willing to fly to your homeland, and really, can you blame them?" The bird looked himself over. "What do you have to lose? Seize opportunities. Or, trust me, you could be here, stuck like this forever."

Pierre and Tiberius surveyed the glistening paradise with dry expressions.

"Where is this Excavation?" Pierre finally asked.

Tiberius smiled. "The South side of Bouvet. Two rises of the sun." Then the albatross turned and painfully limped off.

Despite not having an in-depth conversation with Tiberius before now, Pierre had developed a deep respect for his work and all he risked for his family. Conflicting stories floated around the Cape about how the albatross came upon his strange assortment of injuries. The most popular being he was attacked on the Falklands delivering the message. What faintly stumped Pierre was how he got back so fast from the Falklands in this condition, returning the same day he left? He was a swift albatross, and a powerful flier, but was that really possible?

That mattered less to Pierre in this moment than no one telling him of the Great Excavation. Why didn't they say anything? Were they *trying* to keep him here? With citizens revelling in their new families and elites worried about issues of Cape safety, perhaps it slipped their minds. Regardless, he was glad Tiberius thought enough to tell him. Excitement coursed through his veins as his imagination ran wild. How strangely life can change. The odds were absolutely astronomical. He tried not to think of it. What are the chances he'd come across *anyone* who knows *anything* of value? Still he couldn't help thinking, there was *some* chance. Some opportunity. Some something. Pierre bounced in a joyful gambol. Despite the shattering probability, he still couldn't help thinking. *What if?*

Chapter 35

Impatience can ruin an otherwise good plan. In the span of time following his talk with the albatross, Solus prepared. Everything had to be flawless. The harsh unwavering climate on Bouvet Island had shaved him to a skeleton. Less daunting, more haunting, yet still enraged with the vigor of the condemned. His three pectoral puncture wounds had completely scarred over along with the engravings in his shoulder from Banishment. Solus admired the slightly raised tissue on his chest. This was well earned. Awakened by an epiphany mixed with the fear for his life, the albatross had spilled very pertinent details. Information quivered off his beak and Solus collected every nugget.

For this information, the albatross wanted a trade. His freedom when Solus made his coup. Once the Cape surrendered, Tiberius was promised to be saved and have a place of high regard within the new system. A small sacrifice, Solus thought. And agreed, with the condition Tiberius could perform a singular assignment successfully. After two days, Solus crossed to the other side of Bouvet Island and entered the Great Excavation. He scanned the perimeter and approached a specific section ready to execute his plot.

Chapter 36

As the penguins from Caterwaul arrived and docked on Bouvet, Pierre wiggled himself dry and paused at the edge of the vision. The jagged glacial mountains he remembered from his journey seemed to bisect this island, separating Paul's lonely seclusions from the gaudy, robust attractions of this kind of penguin's world fair. Citizens scattered like silverfish to their individual pleasures, criss-crossing Pierre's path. Pierre lingered, and as he took his first step he felt deep grooves in the ice below his webbed foot. Some kind of icy engraving. He bent over and looked closer. It was a map of some sort. Trampled and ignored by more experienced visitors.

The newbies, which included Pierre, all huddled, necks curved, peering down at the prominent marks in the ice. Lines spread in six directions marking sections of the event: Toboggan Trails (Left), Battle Arena (Diagonal Left), Sea Treats (Straight Left), Wonder Cure (Straight Right), Scavenger Sect (Diagonal Right), Garment District (Right).

A good chunk of the colony was in attendance but the only ones Pierre actually knew were the two he hunted with. His aunt and uncle stayed home, confessing their vacation *was* when half the Cape went on vacation. 'The beauty without the busy,' they called it, even when asked separately. Pierre imagined this was even more true for them now than ever.

Aria opted to remain behind, helping Sachem and Puddles, giving Pierre could have her slot. The official story was she really didn't care for the event like she used to. Pierre thought that only half true, and was very grateful for her generosity.

As Xander impatiently explained en route, the Great Excavation happened once a year. Always after the mating season. The festivities were a privilege not a right and newcomers were required to forfeit their first time to show patriotism. Pierre sensed Xander's aggravation. Pierre was sure in Xander's eyes him being allowed to come his first year was yet another exception applied to this stranger from some faraway place. Pierre thought Xander envied what he did not understand.

With half the Cape coming here at a time, it meant only fifty percent of the provisions were necessary. This was the season for eager trainees in every department to get some field experience. Another benefit to only half the citizens leaving is it kept a populated presence on the Cape. Deterring settlers and squatters.

With access to both forest and ocean, Tree Dwellers, albatross, a controlled point of entry, and scarce natural predators Caterwaul's geography was extremely ideal. Location, perhaps as

181

much as any other factor, likely aided in the building of their great society.

But every society, no matter how great, required an outlet. An unchecked release to peel them away from their typical areas and typical selves. This Excavation was their outlet. The molting of the mundane.

Tiberius said the event lasted two arcs of the sun. Pierre doubted that was enough time to take in all it had to offer. Struggling not to get lost in the bustle and majesty, Pierre planted himself in a busy intersection and got to work digging for information. In a manner of seconds, he had been bumped, brushed, and shoved. Regaining his composure each time, he sighed. Brief gaps between the crowds showed the fullness of the event and it was astonishing.

There were penguins trading strange items, laughter and running, nodding and smiling, varieties of fish and breeds of penguin Pierre had never seen or heard of all set in a large, icy expanse. The soft white snow met the dazzling blue sky created a beautiful backdrop for the festival visited by seabirds of every colony and clan. Waddling bodies swished to and fro. Pierre shook his head and snapped out of it. He pulled himself from the mesmerized stupor. Reciting the purpose for his visit. He continued tirelessly surveying any and every penguin who dared cross his path.

KING PENGUIN

"Do you know anyone who knows about the Falklands? Do you know anyone who's been? Have you even heard of the Falklands? "

Most never looked up. Some rushed by to avoid the conversation. The ones who did take the time to respond didn't always have pleasant things to say about his endless questioning.

Penguins didn't come here to be bothered, or pestered, or dwell on sad wars in sad faraway places. Penguins came to be happy. Easy. Loose. Free. Whatever threatened that notion, like Pierre's war-related interrogation, was likely seen as a violation of that joy and peace.

The day wore on and hope faded with each frustrated shake of the head. Pierre's body felt heavier with each shrug of the shoulder. Each aggravated wave. Penguins rushed by before Pierre could finish his sentence. Those who crossed his path once before went the long way around, circling Pierre like a roundabout, staring at him the entire way. Pierre's throat was dry from speaking. His energy was drained from his muscles. Fatigue settled in and robbed him of his vivacity. His once lively questions shortened in length, and fell in tone. 'Do you know of the war in the Falklands?' dipped to 'The war in the Falklands?' and finally just to 'Falklands?'

The more Pierre asked the more he realized these penguins knew nothing of his home. He was on a fool's errand. This event prided itself on being a meeting of every known colony on Earth and yet was oblivious to the raging war just across the ocean. The continuously blank stares proved to Pierre the world was only what you knew of it.

The King penguin dragged himself to the nearest section of the massive event and collapsed. Gazing at a soft tuft of snow between his short, webbed feet, Pierre looked up to the Macaroni penguin standing above him. Pierre muttered his question.

The cheerful round-faced attendant with crazy golden eyebrows shook his head. He leaned over the small block of rectangular ice he was trading from and began speaking.

"We've got an incredible delicacy this season." The merchant said, arching his golden eyebrows. "A pack of wild penguins from a faraway coast brought us a real treat. Shark meat!"

Pierre squinted and frowned.

"Want to know how they did it?" The merchant continued.

Before Pierre could respond the merchant excitedly continued.

"One penguin lures the shark into an underwater cave, where waiting in ambush is *six* other penguins. Right? Their beaks were been sharpened to spikes. As the shark snaked his way into the cove, The six penguins moved silently." The merchant started to do a weird oscillating body wave. "Once the shark was in and its gills were exposed, they struck! And struck! And lanced and struck and hit and lanced and labalalala." The merchant shook his face furiously, then leaned back. "Until the beast keeled over. Protectionists call these penguins savages. And I call those protectionists self-righteous punks. I," he beat his chest, dragging the vowel, "consider these hunters Penguin-itarians." The Macaroni trained his vision on Pierre's face. "So, you want to munch on a predator?"

Pierre stood to his feet, looking at the assortment neatly laid upon the slab of ice. The merchant's food called to his grumbling stomach. Yet, as he gazed at the piece of grey and pink predator meat something arrested him.

Amongst other things, sharks *ate* penguins. And here he was, possibly out of some form of vengeance or revenge, ready to eat what would've eaten him. But, even in this famished state the question bothered him. *How many penguins did this shark already eat?* Without being able to put it into words, eating pieces of this shark felt kind of like cannibalism. He looked at the meat. Pierre scrunched his face like he tasted something bitter.

"I'll try something else," Pierre said, shaking the thought.

The Macaroni stood tall and lowered his eyes. "Oh. And, what would your expert tastes prefer?" There was salt in his tone.

The wide variety made choosing difficult. Absolutely nothing looked normal about the array of fish. Beige Stargazer, Orange Wrasse, Blue Runner, Green Dragonet, silver Sargo, red Striped Weever, and more varieties that Pierre was just now introduced to.

Being selective suddenly felt important. Pierre rocked his weight side to side. He didn't want to seem ignorant, but so much of what he saw was new to him. Refusing the merchant's offer,

Pierre now felt he was being tasked to make a sophisticated decision on his own. He clinched his jaw. He oddly wanted to prove he wasn't a savage. That he knew stuff. Prove he was sophisticated, classy and complicated. He wasn't. In fact, he was very regular. His favorite meal, Mackerel, was common and base. Yet, Pierre felt like he was being challenged. Like this was a game.

Pierre hovered over the neatly laid collection. He thought and he stared. He stared and he stared. The Macaroni cocked his head to the side and sighed impatiently. Pierre glanced up at the once-bubbly attendant. Then, still looking at the attendant, Pierre pointed down and across his body to the left. The attendant leaned back and winced like now he just tasted something disgusting. Pierre looked at his choice. Black and white Inkfin. The attendant gave a lingering look at the fish. Pierre's gaze nervously darted left and right. Then, deciding to commit to the bluff, Pierre raised his chin and gave a nod. The vendor twisted his face once more, then laughed. Pierre laughed too, though not sure why. The Macaroni then slid the King penguin a half dozen of Inkfin.

"You've made a good choice."

"What do I owe you?"

"My treat. You look beat. Like you need it. This thing is supposed to be about getting closer as penguins just as much as the fun. Though, many forget that and just come for their agenda."

Pierre loosed his shoulders. He nibbled the fish which had a sweet, sharp tang. Exhaling deeply, the food was much needed energy. He looked down blankly. He had learned nothing. The day was a waste. He sat again and was content to settle there, humbled for the rest of the evening and semi-defeated on the cold ground in front of the fish vendor, until something caught his eye. Through quick gaps in the bustling crowd, a sight pulled him to his feet.

Chapter 37

Sudden and unannounced. Abrupt and somewhat rude. If he readied his whole life for this moment, he'd still be grossly unprepared. No matter where in the world this had happened to him the reaction would be the same. He felt guilty. There was so much to do. He turned to walk away. His functions stuck. He went to ask a stranger his usual questions, a polite Rockhopper who actually stopped and addressed him. But all Pierre could say was garbled nonsense. What was wrong? Pierre was completely distracted. What was this, this thing, this, this elixir? Why was it happening now? There couldn't be a worse time.

She turned and caught a glimpse of him staring across the walkway. He ducked. *She saw me*! He wanted to run. Each of his two lousy webbed feet were of no use. She was coming! Why! He looked at his feet again, cursing them. His father's only courting advice echoed in his head. Not because it was good advice, but because it was the only advice he had: 'Start with your left, you'll do your best. Start with your right, you'll be all right.' And what the hell did that mean? Pierre debated which was the better of the two while he moved in a sort of dance. One in front of the other, slow and unsure, before jerking it back and replacing it with the other. Left. Right. Left. No, right. He wore a serious frown. A light voice spoke very close.

"Are you alright?" she asked.

Pierre lifted his head to her shimmering emerald eyes. His verbs hitched. His nouns caught.

"Are you alright?" she repeated in a more concerned tone.

"Aaaahhh," he nodded, staring.

She squinted. "Do you have a condition? What is wrong with your feet?"

"Feet?"

"Your feet!"

Pierre looked down. They were still moving. He snapped them still. *Stupid feet.*

"I was going to bring you to the Medics," she said.

"Medics?"

She looked him up, down, then back up. She motioned for him to follow. Pierre hustled to keep pace. *Now my feet work!* She approached a booth with seven small Fairy penguins which were so alike in appearance they could *be* each other.

"They call this the Wonder Cure section." She said, more to the seven little penguins than Pierre. "Yet every time I come here, I simply wonder why there's no cures."

"So-rry, Em-ily," the workers said in unison like a small band of students.

"We're working on it," one replied, before stepping behind two others.

Pierre assumed this penguin was the leader, for no other reason than at the moment, he happened to be standing in front.

"I know, I know" she said, "I'm just roughing you up a bit. A quip of humor is the only thing that gets me through it, and," she raised a wing, "to not going on a slappin' frenzy. Running through the crowd. Slappin' the face off penguins." Emily started slow-motion running in place. She stopped every few steps to backslap an imaginary, unsuspecting penguin.

Smmmack! What you say?" *Pap-Pap!* Oh, you want some too?" *Hyuh!*

Pierre laughed. Her eyes glinted, telling these fictioned reenactment. This Gentoo penguin was absolutely crazy. And, also, the prettiest thing he'd ever seen.

Pierre managed to talk through a chuckle, finally eeking out more than one word. "Why do you want to slap penguins you don't even know?"

"Because they've have it better than me, and I have to hear them complain about it."

"Mm," Pierre grunted, "I know what you mean."

"Do you?"

Pierre somehow managed to look at her without doing that creepy staring thing he's sure he's been doing until now.

She frowned. "Why are you here?"

"I'm looking for something."

"So am I. So is everyone. *Why* are you here?"

"I have some questions, but no one seems to know the answers."

"Mm," she grunted, "I know what you mean."

"Do you?" He asked

She quickly raised a flipper.

Pierre flinched, then quickly tried to hide the fact that he flinched. "Why are you here?" He asked.

"Solutions. Answers."

"Maybe we can share our questions."

"Or, make up our own answers."

Pierre felt warm blood rush to his face.

"I know what you need," she said, stepping closer.

Pierre swallowed. He looked down and ever so slightly leaned forward.

"Follow me." She said, and whisked away.

Chapter 38

Weaving and slicing through the crowd, they snaked down a path and came to the base of a steep trail. The sparkling snow had webbed footprints mainly going in one direction, with a few staggering prints coming back down toward them.

"Cowards," she muttered, glaring at the downhill prints.

Pierre examined the footprints. Wondering why so many went up, but so few came down. Grey rocks lined the outside of the road bending where the eye could not follow. As he walked toward the sky, the noise he hardly noticed before fell further and further away. Pierre didn't know where he was going or cared. The day rewarded him not for his efforts, and today he had no more efforts to give. Tomorrow, he promised. Tomorrow would be the day. Their conversation was constant. Honest. Easy. Slowly, she got around to lapses in her mother's memory. Slowly, he got around to talking about home. They made their ascent, carried by a surprising exchange.

"Wanna know a secret?" she asked, cutting through Pierre's rant on Mackerel and its glory.

"Sometimes, you don't get an answer or a cure, sometimes you just have to cope."

Pierre opened to address the theory, but in the approaching the summit, the skyline broke. The water looked like a massive pool, clouds crossed the sky in herds as a ball of light shone through splitting itself into smaller parts. A tingling draft brushed over his body. Emily planted one foot in front of the other in an accomplished stance, panting slightly. She stared off into the endless visage as if looking for the face of her maker.

Pierre pulled alongside slightly more winded than he wanted to let on. Water fitness, he learned, was not like land fitness. Running on the remains of a day full of solicitation, the only thing that carried him was the chatter. He stood, poorly erect, speaking through unattractive beak-breathing.

"Or maybe," he finally said, "the merchants, don't have, what you need. Maybe, the answer isn't to stop life, but to find a way, to move with it." He struggled to lift a flipper. "Even when it's hard."

"Easy for you to say," she shot, stepping on his words. "Both your parents are still alive."

"You promise?" He was still unable to catch his breath and still trying to mask it, speaking loud through unattractive beak breathing. This climb was much taller than his perch in Caterwaul.

He plopped down and she followed, her gentle gaze upon him.

"If it's bad, why don't they leave? Are they afraid?"

"Of what they'd leave behind. They believe home is something worth saving."

"A place is only as good as its penguins."

"I believe that too. That's why I want to go back. I'm in this paradise now, you can see it there." He pointed to the two titanic beige mountains, visible across the stretch of water. "No war, no lack of food, I can live as a hero the rest of my life, but I don't want it. Not because I lust for battle or have nostalgia about hunger pains, I miss them. I just miss them. I'd trade these blue skies in an instant."

"Why don't you?"

"They risked a lot to get me away."

"Ah. I don't think you're living in misery so you can be polite. Please. What's the real reason?"

Pierre took a pause. "They depend on me now."

"Who?"

"The colony."

Emily sat back and for a long while said nothing. "Is it better not knowing?"

"I would rather be able to cherish what time I have, than to have none at all."

"At least it comes with hope. The other side of your guess. You can believe what you want. Good or bad. You don't want to see your parents how I have to see my mother. To be in that pain with them."

"I'm not much better without them."

Pierre never had a real talk about home since he was sent away. Short debriefings with those more curious than caring about the facts, but never about the feeling. Possibly, she was the only one who cared.

"Welp," Emily said, hopping to her feet as she stretched her back, "while you're here, in this blissful miserable place, make the most of it." Her pace changed. She swung her flippers, seeming to be in a rush. "Ever been Tobogganing?" Emily glanced down at him.

The wind on the mountaintop now dry and chilling. Pierre stood, peering over the cliff, bending his neck to follow steep curves. Visitors below looked like wandering black specks on a light blue backdrop. "I've seen it done," he said with assurance. He hadn't. But it sounded better than the truth of him being scared pale at the thought. The maniacal first drop made him want to crawl into an egg.

"Good, let's go," she said with a pop.

His eyes bulged. "Oh. No. No, no, no, I—I just wanted to walk you up."

"I walked you up."

"And now I have. Long day. Just ate." He patted his stomach. "Umm. See you at the bottom?"

KING PENGUIN

Emily rolled her eyes. "Sand penguins are such sissyfoots when it comes to the Trails. I don't know wh—Ah!" Emily shrieked, breaking her even tone, lost, gazing over the cliff.

In his cowardly stammer, Pierre had unconsciously inched several feet back. "What is it?" he said in a heavy voice, not budging from his distance.

Emily remained mute, focusing below. She swallowed hard, twisted her face, shaking her head. Pierre moved, sliding his webbed feet along the smooth ice instead of picking them up.

She screamed, pointing down into a swarm of dots. He rushed to her side.

"What?"

"There!"

"Where!"

"There! There! *There!*" She was hopping.

"Where?" he asked, scanning nervously.

"Right…over…there."

Next, Pierre noticed two things. A sharp drop in her voice. And a hard whack at his back. For a full three seconds his entire body touched nothing. He was freefalling parallel to the mountainside. Then his belly bumped against the slope as a smooth arc of ice met his descent. When Pierre found the courage to open both eyes, Emily was at his left. She was rushing down the wide half-pipe with both wings cocked to the side. A small curve appeared ahead through the snowy flurries. Emily leaned in rhythm and zipped around the curve. Pierre hit the bend fast. Wobbling out of control, he tumbled forward helplessly before slamming back onto his stomach. Emily up ahead, gently skimmed her claws atop the ice, and slowed to align with Pierre.

"Drop left foot to go left," she yelled. "Drop right, to—" a whipping wind snatched her words and carried them up the mountain.

Pierre's cheeks felt like they were being blown to the back of his face. He wiggled and swerved, trying to get a hold on the mechanics. Emily quickly lifted her anchors and jetted out in front. Another bend loomed in the distance. Emily took it high, sliding nearly to the top of the halfpipe before slanting down with added momentum. Pierre tried to follow suit. Once he realized how high the slope was he panicked. He couldn't stop.

He dropped a foot in panic, not sure ahead of time which foot. He banked a hard left into the curve and slid limply up the slope before flopping over onto his back. As he lay upside down, tired and out of breath, completely ready to forfeit and go home, he realized, once again he was gaining speed. *Was there no end?*

Pierre accepted his certain doom and braced for the embarrassment to come. Another hard cuve. Another high slope. Another crunch. Another tumble. Another flash of pain. Swaying left to right Pierre tried to roll over. Lifting his neck to see what torment lay ahead he saw the upside-down sky, the distant sea, and...nothing. No left curve. No right curve. No ice. *No Ice!* Pierre managed somehow to flip right-side up, figuring this must be an optical illusion. An eternity away, he witnessed a small beautiful speck be catapulted into oblivion.

Pierre suddenly dropped off another sharp cliff. He flapped his wings tirelessly, hoping they'd catch wind. But the thick condensed flippers were built for water not air. Pierre somersaulted through the air in wild diagonal front flips before another slope came to catch him. A short white ramp lingered up ahead, slightly obscured by the misty grey breeze. Beyond which Pierre saw nothing. Pierre survived a war, a leopard seal, and the D.E.W. cave to be defeated by a beautiful bird who pushed him off a cliff.

The rush to the ramp was merciless. His innards sank. The sky and ocean bled together. Pierre saw one mixed blur as trails of water trickled from the corner of his eyes. Instantly, he couldn't no longer feel the ice running along his belly. When he was brave enough to look down, he realized the ice wasn't there.

Chapter 39

Ground. Slope. Ocean. All three fell away as Pierre launched through cold, crisp air. Instinctively, he flapped his wings again. It was all he could think to do. This time though, it seemed to work. As his ascent slowed he felt he was actually flying! His recurring dream of swimming through the sky had come true. The weightlessness was amazing! Euphoric! Not like thick sluggish liquid, which did everything it could to hold him back. This air was free. Uninhibited. He wished he could feel like this forever.

As the sensations of life resonated at their peak, his ascent slowed. The wind in his ear churned to a stop and took an intermission. Pierre observed a stillness in the world like never before. He closed his eyes, begging for it to stay. But as his beak slowly tilted back down, the Earth snatched in him for a hug. The loud ruffle of air in his ear rose again to a deafening level. He yelled. Hollered. Screamed. Pleaded. Everything below was a bright white. He couldn't make sense of where he was going, or how fast he was going there, or *why* anyone would do this?

KING PENGUIN

'The Toboggan Trails', where penguins come to live one last time before they die. Falling was a lot faster than rising and before he knew it Pierre was wondering where everybody went. Where were the vendors? Where were the visitors? Where was Emily? He then sliced deep into a thicket of colorlessness, as something humongous and soft swallowed him whole. His rapid velocity was pacified into a pleasant tumble, rolling him out the other side of an incomprehensibly massive lot of snow. The commotion of the festival reconvened.

"You okay?" Emily's voice echoed, somewhere nearby.

Disoriented from the dips, whips, turns and drops, Pierre panned for the source. The dizziness ebbed, as three Emilies disappointingly phased into two, then one. Pierre could only hyperventilate and look at her like a cat doused in water. She was a lunatic, getting cheap thrills from unsuspecting sand penguins. Lying there at the base of her rollercoaster, he blinked for long periods of time. Tuning in to the rapping of her foot, Pierre noticed she wasn't sympathetic. She wasn't even apologetic. She was impatient. What was she waiting for? Pierre swallowed hard and then finally shook his head slightly in response to the question posed moments ago of if he was okay. He was okay, but he certainly wasn't going to let her know that. He had a reasonable fear of what she may want to do next.

"Shut up, you liked it," she said, apparently seeing through his facade.

Emily expressed that she had been riding the trails for years when her mother would take her before the illness. She admitted having the same exact look the first time she rolled out of the snow pile. Privately thinking her mom was jealous of her youthful good looks and had plotted to 'off' her on the slopes. But once she came through on the other side frightened, discombobulated, ruffled but ultimately okay she realized she had the best time of her life. Only fear of the unknown that can put that kind of look on a penguin's face. Then she admitted Pierre was right. It is better to know. So, you can enjoy the ride.

"Took long enough getting down here," she said with a sass.

"I'm glad there was a down here," Pierre mumbled, his breaths more spaced out. "I thought I was going to die."

"You are," she offered with a devilishly macabre smile. "Just not yet. Now, come come. *Let's do it again!*"

Pierre jabbered senselessly as his rebuttal was pure mush. Before he knew it, he was being forcefully prodded, waddling back toward the walkway. Grinning slyly like a youth who had just taken a playful beating going back for seconds. Pierre was once that penguin, jumping on his brother's back as soon as he got home from the front lines. Only to have Craig's well-trained reflexes and strong physique hurl him across the cave. Pierre would roll over giggling and come stumbling back for more. The truth was, he did like the Toboggan. It was the most fun he ever had and now, waddling toward the summit was the first time he'd laughed this laugh, light and unrestricted, in quite some time.

In that moment, he grasped the tough decision his parents made to send him away. This was what they were talking about that last night in their cave. This was why they took the risk. For him to be happy. Completely. Since leaving the Falklands, this moment was the first time he happened to be exactly where he wanted to be.

They climbed and fell down the Trails ten times that fateful day, with the newness of what they'd just discovered giving them fresh life. On the last trip up, they paused to watch the sun give its triumphant bow before retiring for the evening. As they sat, breathing in the twilight atop the highest mountain, Pierre never really wanted to come down. A star-covered dome curved around them, and they wrapped themselves in it. They declared softly to one another what they already knew and solidified their bond with a different kind of dance. Pierre Oiseau didn't quite find what he was looking for that day on Bouvet, but when he wasn't looking something found him. Love.

Chapter 40

Morning arrived like a warm alarm. It was the last day of the Great Excavation and in his heart Pierre was still committed to searching, but the vigor he once possessed had greatly waned. That drive now having to share space. His mind wanted desperately to hold on to his past, to the worrying, to the what-ifs, but everything he once felt was mixed with last night. Prying his thoughts from Emily was like taking a fish from Puddles.

The process of waking up that morning was a slow disappointing bloom. The dull orange morning came with a reality. It came with their obligations and circumstances. The tattered series of events which shaped their lives. Truth was, she had to go her way, and he had to go his. Her mother was sick. Families needed him. Emily had already stayed away past her curfew from a mother who lacked total self-sufficiency. Her mission for medicine, again, was unsuccessful. They walked the descent this time. Not taking the slide, but the trail of those Emily once referred to as cowards. He could see something in her eyes, and he knew she could see it in his. They wanted to hide up there. From who they were and who they were supposed to be. Decency and nobility weren't a fair trade. The satisfaction of doing the right thing seemed a frail reward compared to what they just discovered. Sharing that same gaze, the wide-eyed fear gave way to a sagging guilt. They knew they were going to ultimately go and be better than they wished they had to be.

As they walked the wet snow, within its guidelines of rocks, the conversation didn't at all resemble the day before. The communication was mainly without words. They made a covenant up on that mountain, a promise, a pact both felt could not break. He'd found no one like her across the entire sea. Reaching the bottom of the Trail, Pierre noticed they were now officially amongst those who walked back down the mountain instead of taking the slide. Webbed footsteps going against the grain. Emily called the owners of such footsteps cowards. Perhaps she was right. Turning to the left they passed by a long booth Pierre didn't noticed the day before. Pierre took a distracted detour and Emily followed.

"What-can-I-do-for-ya?" a slim Magellanic blurted so fast it all sounded like one word.

It took Pierre a moment to compute. Meanwhile, the keeper looked everywhere but forward.

"I want to get something for my…" Pierre hesitated, then continued, "mate." He wasn't bold enough to check her reaction but in his mind, she may have blushed.

"There is no getting, only winning."

"Winning?"

"Winning."

"How?"

"Riddles."

"Riddles?"

"Is there an echo out here? Riddles."

"Okay."

"Unlike the brutes over at the Battle Arena, bashing their brains out for fleeting machismo, *we* champion intellect."

Pierre opened his beak to speak.

"Yes, intellect," the keeper repeated.

Pierre closed his beak.

"Answer all three riddles, you get a prize."

"What if I answer two?"

"A compliment."

"One?"

"Sarcasm."

"None?"

"Unflappable disrespect. You ready?"

"If I lose can I try again?"

"Maybe if she asks."

Emily leaned forward. "If we lose can we try again?"

"No. Okay, first riddle: There is a word of letters three, add two and fewer there will be."

Emily whispered into his ear, "It's a trick. You can't add to something and have less of it."

Pierre stared. It was tough to concentrate with Emily so near.

"Maybe," Pierre finally said, "the word won't be less, but whatever it's referring to. These things thrive on simplicity. We have to try and think in reverse." Pierre tapped his beak and lifted his head.

"Few."

The attendant looked off. "Huh?"

"Few!"

The attendant narrowed his eyes.

Emily bounced. "Well!"

"Second riddle." the attendant blurted.

Emily wiggled. Pierre bounced up and down.

The attendant cleared his throat then raised his voice. "Ahem. Second. Riddle."

They nodded.

"You heard me before yet you hear me again. Then I die, till you call again."

Being raised in caves Pierre couldn't help but laugh when he thought about an answer. Whenever permitted, they'd howl for evenings, saying absolutely nothing of purpose. He and his brother were fascinated by the strange acoustic response. What lived in those deep dark places repeating whatever you'd say so well you couldn't tell your voice from its? Emily, standing right at his shoulder was standing with a devious smile.

"An echo," Pierre said, lowly.

Emily hopped, brimming with glee. "I've never won! I've never won anything!" she spouted.

The attendant eyeballed her, lifting his chin. "And you still haven't."

"Is it correct?" Pierre said, commanding the bird's focus.

"The true test of a mind is not depth but diversity." The attendant tapped the tips of his wings together, put his chin down in his chest, then looked up. "It's more beautiful and colorful than anything seen, yet no penguin can touch it, not even a King."

Pierre stared at the ice. Emily at Pierre. Their gazes met and his fell back to the floor.

The attendant smiled and leaned forward. "Hmm?" he mocked.

"Um," Pierre said.

"*Hmm!*" The attendant said more forcefully.

Pierre searched his partner.

"I thought so," the keeper said turning around.

Pierre had to say something. They were running out of time. "Sunse—"

"Rainbow!" Emily shrieked.

KING PENGUIN

The attendant stopped and for a long while didn't move. Then, he turned around slowly. "What ridiculous answer did you just give?" He questioned.

"A rainbow," Emily stammered, sounding less sure.

The attendant gazed up into the sky, then shook his head disapprovingly. "Follow me." Parting a troop of ornery seabirds who were standing standing guard about twelve paces behind the attendant, he escorted Pierre and Emily into a private open space.

"Welcome to Scavenger's Spiral," he said, grumbling.

A layout of prizes laid in the snow, curling out from its center like a giant seashell. Giant orangish-red feathers, sparkling blue gems, a massive bronze egg as tall as Pierre, dazzling white cloaks, rare purple flowers, pointed silver sticks, and more. Emily and Pierre walked the wide curved path sprinkled with collector's items as the keeper turned curator, explaining each piece the couple showed interest in. Including the piece's known history, usages, and method of procurement. The quick-tongued Magellanic was a profound database for these oddities of the sea. Emily perused giddily, touching, moving, and tapping things. Sometimes adding the occasional yip. She uttered half-finished sentences, ignoring both Pierre and the attendant as she wandered the exclusive treasured garden. An array of trinkets, each as undiscovered to them as the next.

Pierre browsed the cache, equally impressed as he was ignorant until one stopped him in his tracks. "What is it?" he asked. Emily rushed over to the group.

"This little doo-dad drifted south of the Canary current, then got picked up by the Brazilian current and wound up on the South Georgias. A seabird in our colony, who had done some hard time in an Australian aquarium, said he'd seen visitors carry something like this around their neck. And that's how I think you're supposed to wear it. Around your neck. We've tinkered and played with it for some time and..." He signaled to two workers who picked up the prize without breaking stride and moved toward Pierre. "Slip the loop over your head like so, down to your shoulders." Pierre stooped as they put on the soft, smooth contraption. "Then pull gently with your beak to tighten, and fix this loose part here."

"Why anyone would wear such a thing is lost on me, but that's how he said he'd seen it done and we can't figure any other use for it. So, dagnabbit I guess that's how it's done!" The security crew moved away. Once adjusted it looked like a golden butterfly with its wings spread wide was sitting atop Pierre's chest.

"It's beautiful," Emily said.

"But I came to win *you* a prize."

"I don't need two prizes." Emily said, and turned to the curator. "We'll take this one."

Before the group dispersed, Pierre had them remove the reward and give it to his partner. He had to stay with the Cape, and she

209

had to stay with her mother. While they were held in separate worlds, this would be a token of their promise. They then resolved to meet every Excavation. Pierre didn't care about the colony's 'rotation rule'. He was coming. He walked her to the departure point for Antarctica and they rubbed their cheeks together in silence. As she took her leave Pierre sank. He smiled. He felt he made his peace.

Wandering back through the maze, he worked his way to the other side of the island. From a rest area near the Garment District, a familiar sound buzzed as Pierre moved through the scattered assembly which gave him no choice but to pause. He shook his head and continued. The sound buzzed again, this time stopping him in his steps. It hung. Unmistakable. Impossible for him to ignore. Syllables he thought he'd never hear. *Falk-lands*.

Chapter 41

Pierre twisted and turned following the words. He listened. Hoping to check fact against his imagination. He moved forward toward two penguins talking. He stopped and listened again. Then, stumbled drunkenly into their conversation. One was talking very loud, while the other seemed only half-care about the exchange. Pierre, on the other hand, was drawn majestically.

A penguin stood in front of him now with shades of grey, purple, and black orbiting his body. He was draped in elaborate, colored seaweed wraps from the Garment District within the festival. Wearing such dazzling hues, Pierre assumed he was here to find a match. The stranger's speech pumped with excitement, as his words bounced and rolled. The top half of his back was crouched over and his neck slung long and low causing him to look up at penguins he otherwise would've been taller than if he could stand straight.

"Did you say Falklands?" Pierre asked, interrupting what was appearing now more of a monologue.

The colorful bird turned around cautiously in more steps than it should take anyone to do so and fixed his focus on the King. "I did. Do you know of the place?"

"I'm from there," Pierre said, sticking out his chest before sucking it back in a little.

"Yea? Are you the fellow who's been asking about the place?" the stranger questioned with a smile.

"I am," Pierre said, excited that his interrogations finally yielded fruit.

"Come closer my dear so I can get a closer look at you." The hunched bird circled Pierre like a specimen. "Right height." *Mumble-mumble.* "Right weight." Mumble. Mumble. He looked up from under Pierre's chin. "Right kind." He shuffled back for a full view. "By golly, you *are* him. Delio, ecstatic to meet you, you're just as he described!"

"Who?"

"Paul Jaunty of course."

"You know Paul?" Pierre yipped, flinging his beak over both shoulders. "Is he here?"

"You know he's not one for crowds."

"He *saved* me!"

"So I've learned."

"I should visit him before I leave!"

"No, no. He's resting. I stopped by his place on the way in and he was insistent that if I happened to see you I was to tell tell you something about something."

The stranger looked up and to the left, as if trying to read bits of memory in the sky. "What *was* it?"

Slowly. Unsteadily. The stranger pulled something from his mind. "He knows I'm terrible with these sorts of things but he insisted. The core...hold on...wait...the poor... the poor, the poor! No. The war...no...if...um. Shoot. Ah. The war. There it is. The war...is. The war is something. The war is colder? Older? No! The war. *The war is over!* You can go home."

The words showered Pierre's body with tingles. He staggered backward. Then, crept forward. He begged the stranger to repeat. The second time, it came without pause.

"This is the same Falklands we're talking about? My Falklands?" Pierre questioned.

"Is there another?" The stranger asked earnestly.

"And the same Paul Jaunty?" Pierre had to be sure.

"Short? Round? Grumpy? Alone?" The stranger asked.

Pierre couldn't believe it. It was really too good to be true. *He could go home.*

"*AHHHHHHHHHHHHHH!*" Pierre yelled accidentally in the stranger's face. "Sorry! Sorry! Sorry. Thank you. Thank you! Thank—You have no ide—I can't—ahp!"

"Mmm hmm. My pleasure," the stranger said, grinning.

213

Chapter 42

When Patricia first discovered her nephew was going to the Great Excavation, she thought it'd be therapeutic. A much needed break from Caterwaul's weighted responsibility. She hoped he'd find answers. Get information. Learn something to tide him over while he accepted this place as the better home.

Patricia knew news from the Falklands never really changed. Even before Pierre was hatched, there was always *some* degree of danger, some ceaseless risk, some big threat which didn't rest or sleep. That's why she left. Because some cycles never end, at least not in one's lifetime. She didn't expect history to actually change, but she did her best to maintain some optimism at least for Pierre and her brother's sake.

To willingly accept a new place as home gives the subject a feeling of power over the process. It helps you feel less out of place. *You* give *yourself* purpose, freedom and permission to claim it. Patricia went through this process when she first got here and she wanted this so desperately for Pierre. For him to gain clarity and contentment, but above all acceptance.

But when her nephew came back from The Great Excavation, this was not what he returned with. Her nephew sprinted through the mountains absolutely ecstatic. Collecting her, the Sachem, and the crew of Catchers, and ushering them to the shore.

Aria stood in their imperfect circle with a stone expression as Pierre told the story in big animated gestures. Xander grinned. Cole blinked. The Sachem frowned. And Puddles just looked. Aria questioned how the Cape would compensate for this loss so quickly. Patricia prodded and tested the information. She wanted to know more. Verify the intel. Find out if what this bird said could really be true. But with Tiberius grounded, what other sources of information did he or they have? This was their only source of news. Her nephew was technically an adult now, with the passing of this recent mating season. Patricia was a skeptic by nature, but if he could go home, if even an ounce of that was true, what could she do? He had to at least go see if this was true. Her duty as an aunt was to keep him safe and provide shelter until he could return. That was the commitment she made to her brother and his mate.

As Safety of the Cape, she had a separate commitment. "Pierre, come here," she said, speaking over some less significant crosstalk. She ushered her nephew away from the crowd. She looked over her shoulder back at the group, most of them still arguing about what was the proper response and plan of action. Aria looked over nervously at them.

"What is it?" Pierre said.

215

Patricia took a long pause. Then parted her beak.

"I know you're excited. But I can't let you leave. That came out wrong." Patricia shook her head. "I mean, you need to stay. We need you to stay. What I'm trying to say is, we need time."

Pierre turned his head, gazing out upon the sloshing ocean of the dark, moonlit sea. It appeared to be a dark purple with soft yellowish twinkles. "Time?" He said, appearing tense. He took a long pause. Patricia was tempted to speak. He sighed and softened a bit. "How much?"

Patricia searched the sand, doing some mental math. "Fourteen. Fourteen sunrises?"

He softly shook his head. Patricia refused to acknowledge the motion. She couldn't. Pierre's silences made the tension thick. He didn't agree to this. He only agreed to do his best while he was here. Patricia suddenly felt uncomfortably warm. "You don't owe us. But."

Pierre exhaled and walked down the shore. She started to follow, then stopped. She drew a breath to say his name, but thought better of it. Standing where Pierre was standing moments ago, she felt something soft and plush curve beneath her foot. She stepped back. It was two of Pierre's feathers in the sand between his webbed footprints. Patricia hunched over and brushed the pebbles away. She moved herself out of the path of the light. She saw what it was. Her eyes swelled. She panted. Patricia was short of breath.

Chapter 43

Things were going better than planned. After Pierre's departure from the Great Excavation, Solus perused the mound of scraps hoarded at the Scavenger's Section, and spotted something of real value. He mumbled to himself, stalking over to indulge the attendant. Solus rattled off answers to the riddles with lightning speed until the quota was reached.

Once the wall of guards cleared and he was let into the spiral of treasures, what the attendant offered him some a twig or branch of some sort, supposedly special for healing. The vendor promised with this supposedly came a sense of wholeness and rest. Solus scoffed at the sheer ridiculousness. No branch or twig or living thing could give him that. He waved it away and he bent to examine something more fitting. Something which could be an extension of his force. A representation of his might. His pulse quickened. The crew came and fastened his prize.

A strange, curious contraption from a more ancient part of the world. Supposedly, where penguins fought penguins for blood sport. The heavy item fitted loosely. Designed for an even bigger foot than his. It drooped heavily when he lifted it up above the ground. He stuck his foot out. The metal contraption clanged and jingled in the wind. Semi-rusted iron glinting in the dull grey light. Solus dragged his reinforced talons across the solid ice, making deep, jagged grooves effortlessly.

"Oh, yes!" Solus grinned. "This will do just fine."

Chapter 44

Hobbling down a sandy stretch of the Cape, Tiberius worked around a bend and ducked out of sight. Patricia smiled, watching him from a distance, thinking of his indomitable spirit and knack for exploration. It's what he'd been doing his whole life, she thought, and even in his throbbing, hurting condition, the large bird simply refused to be tied down. Now he got to explore his home in a different way. While Tiberius has been in recovery, Patricia made it a point to maintain him as the keeper of her secrets. He was still her private vault. He never wanted his life to lack purpose. He was the only one she could talk to and trust he could handle the burden. Patricia still talked. Tiberius still listened. They became very close. After all, what are friendships if not time and trust? Just to share some the weighted information and say it out loud, somehow went a long way to lighten the load. The duo shared something which was theirs alone. A club, for members only. No one else.

The good news was that the Medics said, in time, with continued care, his wounds would heal. But her biggest fear was that something may happen to her or Pierre while Tiberius was injured and there would be no to deliver this news to her brother. This thought, of her dying alone faraway, was ultimately what led to the beginning of their partnership. Amongst the fresh litter of Trans-Atlantic albatross she observed that season, she plucked Tiberius from the last remaining lot of his peers. He was awkward for sure. Obtuse. He had a gangly frame which proved far too much for him to manage gracefully. It was hard even watching him walk, and the other young albatross mocked him for his disproportions. Snickering in private, and sometimes in public about his crooked gait.

As a shaky-legged newbie, Tiberius Flock couldn't plant half a dozen steps before tripping over his own appendages. Not helping were his long wings which drug the ground, and his thick heavy beak that tipped him forward as his large floppy feet slapped the sand like a walrus. There was every reason imaginable *not* to pick him. 'Deformities on all accounts' other penguins would say. Patricia realized he was born special. Forged for a very specific calling. Following her heart and instincts, she believed in him when no one else did. Convinced, that with proper nurturing, the objects of his then ridicule could become tools for his glory. As he grew into his own, other penguins who selected from the same lot grew embittered by the missed opportunity. Tiberius was the best flier in the Cape. Some even say ever in Cape history. Other citizens tried to recruit him and convince him to take on side-missions while he wasn't in use for Patricia. They offered him better housing, better treatment and less work. He never took them up on their solicitations. This made her feel special. They *chose* to care for one another. Creating the type of bond which could only be accomplished through free will.

As Patricia stood, staring in a daze toward the area Tiberius disappeared, a citizen zigzagged into her vision. The penguin moved as briskly. Her short body was bumbling down the Cape. Patricia sighed. Penguins like Ethell were the bane of public service. Another sighting. Patricia geared up for the typical routine.

One. Inform: Solus has been Banished, and thus, could not be here.

Two. Condescend Gently: I doubt you saw what you think you saw. It's a common mistake.

Three. Console: Just to be sure I'll send someone to check it out, okay?

Since Banishment, Solus had become the local boogeyman. An urban legend. Their very own phantom. Opportunistic parents used him as a fear tactic to drum obedience out of their fledglings. 'If you don't go to bed...if you don't eat your fish...if you don't pay attention in Academy...the big, Banished penguin will come get you.' Adolescents told tall tales of his alleged horrid crimes at night by the shore. Scaring each other in some sort of cult. Citizens, young and old, claimed to have caught flashes of him in different places around the Cape. Yet each investigation, each

221

thorough check, revealed the culprit to be nothing more than a shadow or rock. Patricia's patience was waning.

The chances of Solus even being alive right now were notably slim. The markings in his shoulders were universal symbols of the condemned constructed long ago at the Great Excavation. Solus wouldn't be able to access any known colonies. Not to mention bodies of the four previous exiles have all spotted by Trans-Atlantics in commute within seven days of the penguin's dismissal. The bodies were opened, rotted, or frozen stiff. What each of the exiles failed to realize was in here, they were protected. In here, they were looked out and provided for, granted shelter and the benefit of institutions. Given the privileges of a good society, so long as they did their part. *Out there*, there was no such agreement.

Even the most malicious, the ones discovered of torture, consistent violence, and murder quickly learned that the open world was no place to be alone. And there was always something more dangerous than you.

The flailing penguin was now close. "I saw him!" the frazzled elder shouted, finally reaching Patricia. "Again! I saw him again!" The bird stood wide and leaned far back for air. "This time, I'm sure! You have to send someone."

As the hearer of all Cape fears, Patricia learned to approach their problems by probability. Evidence of Solus' existence or resurgence physically wasn't there. Every hunt, every search did nothing more than remove valuable Preservers from their posts. Despite the in-depth bird-hunts not a trace had been found to support the claims. Why would Solus risk his life? Patricia wanted to ask, but refrained, knowing it would be considered snide. Out there, maybe he could outlast his predecessors. Figure something clever before something found him, but there was no hope in here. He would be recognized instantly. He would be rushed instantly. He would die instantly.

Still, logic aside, every claim must be adequately looked into. Being responsible for Cape safety meant Patricia had to reserve room for her being wrong.

She veiled her annoyance with a smile. "Okay, Ethell, I'll have someone check it out."

Ethell nodded, and walked off muttering.

"Another one?" Ferdinand asked, walking up with Pierre as they passed by Ethell.

"The more penguins *talk* about seeing him, the more they do."

Pierre leaned in. "Who?"

His aunt and uncle consulted one another with a gaze.

"Solus," she answered.

"The Banishment your very first day," Ferdinand added. "Some think...he's back."

Chapter 45

True evil comes in many forms. Costumed in wrap from the Garment District, Solus was flawlessly cloaked at the Great Excavation. The symbols and scars on his wings and chest were buried deep under the layers of seaweed. Avoiding the few Cape natives who might recognize him was simple enough. Probably, because no one suspected his presence or assumed he had been killed by natural order. The citizens came to Bouvet unaware of the threat which mingled between them. To others, his eyes were a cool and curious feature, a carnival trick, or some deathly sickness. Some marveled, some looked apologetic, but with most of the penguins of the known world present, Solus was hardly the only unique bird.

Currently perched atop a hill, Solus peered down on the commotion below. Solus had stripped himself of his colorful disguise. Bearing his fully marred body. *He had the most notorious face in Caterwaul. The disguise will do him no good here.*

Wiggling the new trinket on his right foot, Solus waited patiently for his accomplice.

"I can't lie," the albatross said, out of breath from climbing the steep ascent, "I was very surprised to see Pierre walk back through those mountains. I thought the whole point of me getting him to go to the Great Excavation was so you could get rid of him."

"I did get rid of him," Solus said, not turning to greet his informant, "and your freedom is on the horizon."

"How can I be free? Nothing has changed!"

Solus made a half-turn. "Something has changed. You thought I was going to kill him. That's short-sighted. Lacks clairvoyance. His death would be a distraction, an unwanted pull. Citizens would rally, be pulled closer together by their loss. They would mourn their beloved. Still reject me. Maybe some would guess it was me. No. That wouldn't work. We want them vacant. Ready to accept their once-neglected son returned to save the Cape in it's time of need. Even if they don't like it. That is what we desire. Willful submission. Abject humility. The strongest push to obedience comes from gratitude. Something I'll have in abundance once I save this overpopulated colony from starvation. Once I spare their young. Once I prevent the second Lack. I will *be* their savior."

Tiberius lingered a few steps back from the Fiordland. "But Pierre seems so healthy, so normal. Better than normal actually, he's happier than ever."

"Good."

"If you didn't kill him, then what *did* you do to Pierre on that island?"

"I infected him with something. Something which when used properly can be the most toxic substance there is. He thinks his family wants him. That they've sent for him, that the war is over, and his dreams have come true," Solus chuckled. "Silly penguin."

Tiberius searched the ground. "The war is worse than ever. You know that. *I've told you that.* Penguins are dying all over the place, he'd barely be able to swim in alive."

Solus smiled. "Exactly. Let the foreigners take care of their own. Leaving our penguins here as a blank slate. Free to worship and soak in our new order."

"What if he survives?"

"If he does somehow manage to make it across the danger-filled Atlantic and evade that death that is so thirstily waiting for him. If he can manage to leave his family in that condition, and come back here. Then we'll kill him. But I think the moment he sees his family. The moment he sees how bad things are for them is the moment he'll abandoned Caterwaul forever."

Tiberius paced back and tucked his bandaged wings close as he could.

Solus stepped toward him. "Ask yourself something. Why are you here?"

Tiberius made eye contact, then glanced away. He frowned. "I was tired of not making my own choices. Always under someone else's rule and schedule. My entire life, measured by subservience. Getting to listen but never speak. Deprived of a break or even the option to fly somewhere for myself. I was concerned that when I died, I'd have no memories of my own making. I suppose, I want to be free."

Solus grinned. "And did you ask the citizens for these things?"

"I suppose, I thought I shouldn't have had to."

"Mmm," Solus mused. "To do what you want, when you want, without consequence. Freedom. You yourself told me how Pierre dropped from one position and picked up another. How freely he went to the Great Excavation when it wasn't even his turn. Could you do the same?"

Tiberius sighed, looking as if he doubted Patricia would grant the permission.

Solus nodded firmly. "You can never be free while he is here. You would've run errands for him and his family 'til the day you died and possibly even after that. There needs to be a new way of doing things. A new way of seeing things. Trust me, I know. I was Banished for exercising my freedom. For doing what was so very important to me. So, bury that remorse, albatross. You've made the only selection."

Footsteps came trudging up the sand. A face scrunched following the two very different prints in the sand which lead to the peak.

"Hey!" A large Preserver said. "You're *not* supposed to be here!" The Emperor rushed up the hill closing in fast on Solus.

Solus lunged forward with the sharp attachments fitted to his claws and sank them deep into the chest of the strong Emperor. Lancing again and again until the bird was no more. The talons dripped with blood. Sand stuck to the thick liquid. Solus exhaled with a quiver. Then, bent his neck to the left.

"If he could find us, so can the rest. I'll find another location until the time is right."

Brushing past the body, Solus etched down the hill with Tiberius not far behind.

Chapter 46

Soft starlight illuminated the five faces in the night. The Sachem cleared his throat. "When Solus was young, he would catch fish. Big fish. The biggest his beak could carry, and drag them back to the Cape. He would toss it ashore and...after a moment, slowly bend each of its fins until it popped and broke. He'd use his claws to cut off the tail and rake scales off its body. As the fish lay there, eyes bulging, mouth agape, deep gashes stretching along its side, Solus would step back and watch. Denying it release, instead just standing there, as if wanting to see how long it could live in pain, suffocating and hurt, squirming before it would submit. Before it would give in to exhaustion and the inevitable. Before it would welcome the end. He'd hunch over, whispering under his breath, *"Maintenant tu sais comment je me sens. Or, now you know how I feel."*

Pierre felt the blood leave his face.

"After getting kicked out of the Builders sect," the Sachem continued, "he ended up here as a Catcher. His anger and rage were powerful fuels for a hunter and made Solus the best we'd ever known, before you. The Cape flourished in his harvest. Families reproduced rapidly, and, no one ever thought to worry."

Aria's gaze fell.

The Sachem peered over and sighed. "Until the disappearances. Mornings became half-days, half days became full, then days on end. Solus was nowhere to be found as crowds slept around the reserve waiting their fill. Production collapsed in every department as doctors and builders, teachers and guards could focus on little more than the famished quake rumbling inside of them.

We tried to help. Working ourselves to the point of prostration, and every time we'd drag ourselves from the ocean, slightly disoriented, the crowd was so large we thought we were hallucinating. Seeing double. They lingered, famished with long gazes. That's when we saw it. He was the heart of our entire colony. We hunted exhaustively, but without his help we simply couldn't meet the need. There were too many. Citizens began to fight over who could eat first. Seniority, occupation, status, popularity, all of a sudden mattered. It was—"

"I took the responsibility," Patricia said, raising her head, "to protect them from threats inside and out. And this certainly fell in that category, but I didn't know how to protect them from this. Their questions turned to suggestions, before long, they were commands. Birds were shriveling in front of us and they wanted to know what I would do, demanding a solution to the death toll.

What could I do, besides wait for it to balance out? Until the number of penguins matched the food. I saw this place becoming the Falklands. I'd never felt so helpless. I knew how to do all these things, but none of them could help me. We tried talking to Solus, bargaining for his aid. Explaining how his negligence was killing us. That we needed him, depended on him. But he was so pumped on his own hubris he didn't feel he had to listen to anybody. We had a part in that. The more I thought, the more I wanted to know. Where was he going? What was so important that he'd risk our lives, the lives of those at the Cape, to get there? Well, one day, I had him followed. Preservers tracked him far out in the ocean and deep into the lower abyss, where they lost the trail. They waited above for Solus to resurface, but he never came up. Or, they didn't see him, or somehow he came up after they left. According to the Wellness Ward, some part of this story makes sense. In his last days, Solus was undergoing an adaptation for creatures of the deep to help them see better in the dark. On the carcass of a fangtooth fish, the Medics said to have found gel in the place where the eyes should have been. The gel was still glowing slightly, which is why the strange fish was brought to them in the first place. The mixing process of the gel with the eyes seemed very painful, but once complete, they think the body's natural heat acted as an energy source. The gel would glow so long as the host body had heat. The ending result is the luminous glow of the eyes. When Solus finally

231

returned to the Cape, we knew where he had been, but more practically where he hadn't. Solus' Banishment was scheduled."

Pierre stiffened.

Aria's brow tensed so tightly it trembled. "He was the reason for everything. When I look back on my life every significant moment, every meaningful decision was because of him. The Lack changed my path. He taught us loss, pain and new fear. This version of me is his creation. As is this version of Caterwaul."

Chapter 47

Not long after the unnerving discussion, the fiery giant rose from his slumber. Pierre was waiting anxiously, as sunrays bled over the ocean. The day had arrived. An orange glow climbed him from foot to face. As it did, Pierre couldn't help but think for a moment if he was making the right decision involving Emily. He would still make the journey every Great Excavation but he knew simply walking out of the Falklands would be much more difficult than walking out of Caterwaul. The dilemma tore at him. His dry, sleep-deprived eyes squinted in the sunrise.

"Who needs you more?" he asked himself. It was an impossible question. His mother and father? His mate? The Cape?

At this point he wasn't sure. He wanted them all somewhere in his future and trying to prioritize was absolutely maddening. The frothy waves he gazed out upon offered no wisdom.

For the Cape, the two last weeks preparing for transition had gone as well as they could. Forcing the colony into impassioned think-tanks on creative sustainable solutions. They pooled every resource, trying to restructure their division of labor to accommodate the food-supply system. The New Plan took advantage of the tireless youth. Instead of delaying them with long training cycles, the Cape gave them opportunities to contribute to the catch earlier and more often. The Sachem outwardly objected to the program, saying he didn't like the danger it placed on the youth and future generations. But the way Patricia viewed it, the need outweighed the risk. Sheltering them was both impractical and dangerous. They needed to make up in numbers and attempts what they didn't have in experience or skill. The consensus was that some would be drafted into the profession, instead of choosing a profession of their own will.

While everyone would be given an educational foundation, being required to serve in the hunt first was mandatory before possibly moving to their preferred role. Lastly, in a state of emergency, the order in which they would be drafted to hunt was agreed upon as follows: Builders, Instructors, Medical, Preservers, then D.E.W.

With these untested theories hanging over the atmosphere there was a nervous hush. What if it didn't work? What if they were sending away young hunters to die? What if parents refused to send their youth into the water. How would the draft be enforced? By begging? By bargaining? By force? The thoughts swam through Pierre's mind, knowing how quickly a division can swell. He was concerned these tough choices may divide the colony. Nevertheless, this was it. The last day he could help with or delay these problems. He had to trust they'd do their best, and remind himself that this place existed long before he did. His aunt already assured him, no matter how it turned out, she was with the Cape. She wasn't running. Not again. This was her home, and this time she was going to fight for it.

From atop the hill, Pierre watched the citizen foot traffic flow in a single direction. The benediction was here. A colony-wide break from duty was taken, as citizens came to hear his final words. Pierre thought this was too much fuss for him. And the citizens would be better off focusing on the future. But his aunt insisted.

Pierre rose, shaking the sand from his body, brushing the tiny pebbles which pressed little dents in his flesh from the prolonged sitting. Pierre walked up to the assembly as Patricia topped the small mound of sand at the foot of the entrance to the colony. "Settle in and listen up everybody!" Patricia called the penguins into order.

As they quited, his aunt let out a slight huff, and cleared her throat. "We are gathered here today to celebrate a very special contribution from one of our newer citizens. Though only with us a short a time, his impact will be felt for generations to come. So, before you have a fun-filled day enjoying the full families and houses we now have, I wanted to give Pierre the opportunity, to say a few words."

Pierre stepped from the audience. Turning to face the crowd, he stopped. He suddenly lost his words. The once manageable population had grown into a massive metropolis, with penguins spread from mountain to sea and D.E.W. cave all the way to the Academy. Lingering on the platform where he once witnessed a Banishing, Pierre slowly addressed the crowd below:

"Um," he stuttered, "I have to leave now."

"Speak up!" a voice cried in the back. "We can't hear you!" shrieked another.

"I have to leave now." His now deeper voice echoed and carried, delivering the news. "I'm leaving behind more than you know. When I came here, I only cared about what I was going through. What I had been through. But I saw, I'm not the only one with hardships. I not the only one with valid pain. I didn't grow up here, young and curious like most of you but I did *grow up* here. That makes this more than a place. I've felt a responsibility to you, for you and that makes you more than just acquaintances."

"Then why the hell are you leaving?" another voice bellowed from the crowd, full of anger, before being audibly shushed by others nearby. Pierre searched the mass. Maybe this penguin said what others had too much decency and civility to verbalize. His conscience clenched. His heart grew warm. "Everyone here is somebody's family. As...as am I. And I want to thank you for being so—"

"Don't leave us!"

"—Supportive. I know change can be scary. Trust me. Everything I'd known was shifted when I was first sent here.

236

Inside, I was confused and angry. I felt alone and hopeless. But I've learned there is no growth without change. Me leaving will mean change for the both of us. I hope you can see your strength more than your hurt. Your purpose, more than your pain. I wish I could tell you challenges won't come. That wouldn't be very true for you or me. What I can show point to is what you've built without me through your own will. A society of Builders, Catchers, Teachers, Preservers, Medics, and D.E.Ws. I have confidence. Rooted not in hope, but in history. We've both been here before. On the edge of scary possibilities. We've had the shore torn from beneath our feet, and been asked, somehow, to survive. Knocked from bliss with such force we thought it was gone forever. Yet, it wasn't gone forever. We have been restored. We have proven we are strong. Not weak. We are not victims. We have the ability to protect our joy. So nothing will *ever* take it again!"

The crowd paused, seemingly processing the words, then brayed with loud voices raising their beaks to the sky. The sound of slapping flippers travelled through the colony.

Patricia moved next to Pierre. "Go!" she said, speaking to the crowd, with a twinkle in her eye. "Celebrate! Celebrate your new joy! Celebrate your new families!"

The citizens dispersed in wide batches. Patricia turned to face Pierre.

"You've grown nephew. You're not our *Pee-Pee* any longer."

237

KING PENGUIN

Pierre chuckled wearily and looked to his aunt. He was grateful for how she'd pushed the colony cheer this transition and see it as a celebration of what they have rather than grieving, angry, embittered exodus. She encouraged citizens to wield their destinies. Build a better system relying on their resources, so no singular penguin could ever threaten the system again.

Patricia leaned over, watching innumerable splashes decorate the ocean. "Whether they know it or not, they *are* actually better off. We did this. We built this colony. We set the rules in place. It's our creation. Our responsibility. It is time we start acting like it." She smiled. "We had to overcome so much, somewhere it was lost that our greatness isn't really in our achievements but our ability to achieve."

Pierre nodded, feeling a little less heavy. As the gay stampede rushed into the breaking waves, a single body remained.

Chapter 48

"How *dare* you pick up and leave like this!" Sherri growled, the hot-blooded D.E.W stomped up to the base of the small hill.

"What're you talking about?" Pierre asked cautiously.

"This is abandon. This is neglect. This is an outrage. And you do it with a smile." She narrowed her gaze. "I won't celebrate this. There's no honor in what you're doing. No selflessness in it at all. "

"Sherri, what are you *talking* about?" Pierre asked, befuddled.

"You know exactly what I'm talking about! Look at you. Running off. Shirking your responsibility just so you can go be young again. So you can go be a fledgling. You know, I oughtta whoop yo—" Sherri trudged up the hill.

"Sherri!" Patricia cut, stepping in, "it is his decision."

Sherri stopped and snarled like a hyena turned away by a lion. "If that's how little you care," she said, staring past the Safety, "then it is best you go." Sherri pounded off to her cave, throwing looks of disgust over her shoulder.

"It's a good thing, Sherri!" Pierre said, somewhat timidly, to Sherri marching away.

"Good for who?" Her small voice shouted back from afar.

Pierre could only guess Sherri's tirade was regarding her concern for the eggs. She was scared. Nervous. Worried. Maybe paranoid about what him leaving could mean for the eggs.

Ferdinand walked up to Pierre's opposite side. "That Sherri must've gotten a little sweet on you during your time together, ey." He hummed a laugh. "*Ey?*"

Aria quietly joined as well.

"You can't expect everyone to be happy you're leaving." She muttered.

Besides the Great Excavation, the two of them spent nearly every day together since he arrived. Hunting and otherwise. She checked his playful ego whenever it reached critical mass, and gave him words of encouragement whenever he felt really sad about home.

Pierre was thankful for her. She, more than anyone, made him feel less alone. In the last fourteen days he noticed she was acting weird. Coming by more. Looking him in the eye more. Like she was now. Lingering after conversations. Wanting to talk about more than work and the world that surrounds it, but thoughts and ideas. What we wanted from our future. Feelings. Her gaze, became noticeably less rigorous and concentrated, shifting into something less threatening, bashful even. Glancing away whenever their eyes met. It was very confusing.

"Are you sure the Cape is ready?" Pierre turned to his aunt.

"Yes. We've held you long enough."

"You think I'm doing the right thing?"

Patricia looked him over, glancing at his stomach. "There are certain situations, Pierre, where even I can't tell you what to do. You're grown now. You have tough choices. All I can say, even though it sounds hypocritical, is consider your family first."

Pierre felt he understood. In the end, this had to be his choice. Despite the Cape's insistence, he took nothing from the Reserve for his journey. He vowed to catch his own fish. Pierre said his goodbyes and stepped backward between the two titanic mountains through which he first came.

Far away on a hill, red eyes trailed Pierre for several moments until he was out of sight. With most everyone enjoying themselves far out at sea, this was the time. Solus descended from his seclusion and entered the Cape.

Chapter 49

"Word around the Benguela is you're in need of a new Catcher?"

Patricia's body stiffened. Aria and Ferdinand had since wandered off. The voice cold and chilling came from the shade between the mountains. She frowned without turning around. "Not like you." He was only a few feet away, but she hoped he would advance, giving her the opportunity to set aside diplomacy and lay him out cold.

Solus was in breach of his Banishment but she was technically no Preserver. There was a need for checks and balances. So the Preservers could prosecute her like any other citizen and she could investigate any inappropriate behavior within the division. Politics here called for the appropriate course of action. If the Fiordland wasn't threatening her life the most she could do was call the Preservers who have the right to execute immediate justice. As the matriarch of this community, one of the aggravating confines was that she, of all penguins, had to display restraint when it was not easy. If any one citizen, including her, could become executioner at their discretion, the Cape could easily slip into anarchy. Patricia grasped the importance of her poise, but she burned with desire in its purest form to bludgeon him until his bones cracked.

"You have no choice," Solus added with a smug twinge in his dry tone.

"Not many options, but there's always a choice. We're ready to take the mantle."

He blurted, "Oh yes, the *Tee*-Waddlers. Who've never been on a real hunt in their lives? They're supposed to help support this entire Colony?"

"Everyone's new at some point. What they lack in skill they'll make up for with persistence. They know what's at risk. We don't need you."

"Oh, Patricia," he uttered, "how vain your optimism can be. Do the numbers. Even with five rotations six times a day they still can't give the Cape what it needs. You know as well as I do that was just a plan to pacify the ignorant. A tactic to delay panic while you scraped together a real answer. But solemnly, you already know the answer. Whether you like it or not I'm all you have. The only legitimate course."

Patricia frowned. The plans of what Caterwaul would do after Pierre left was privy only to a few. *How did he know?*

Of course, she had her concerns whether the Tee-Waddlers were ready. The magnitude of responsibility was unfair for a bird at any age but especially the young and untrained. The times

243

required it, demanding they be more than they were, but she couldn't be sure they could answer the call. True, the Cape could use someone of Solus' capabilities. Until they got set. But not Solus. Clenching her jaw, she turned and glared at him silently. She sensed the bulging muscles protruding from her face.

Solus spoke. "It's not about us or them. Rules or customs. Systems or Banishment. It is about survival. On the cusp of turmoil, will you make the correct decision or the appropriate one?"

"Solus, we hate you."

"Ditto. There's no sense hiding true emotion, but is that worth dying for? Those feelings will pass. Aided along by full bellies and happy families. The scar tissue between us will heal. The skin will regain its color. In time it can be right, and that's exactly what I can give them, what I can give you. Time. Privately, you know this. It's why you haven't called for a Preserver, why you haven't yelled for help."

"I haven't called for help because I don't need any. I want this fight. But your debt is a debt which cannot be repaid."

Solus took half a step forward. Patricia dropped one foot back, locking into a calm, ready stance. Solus was still covered in the shadow of the mountains. His red eyes glowing like small, floating orbs of fire. "Tell me, Patricia, O 'Safety of the Cape,' what will you say when the first of them start to go? Knowing you could've done something and did nothing. What will you say to the mothers and new orphans? What will you tell your albatross, your partner, yourself? That you did all you could when you did not. That *you* made the hard choices? This is the hard choice. The only choice. Not everything can be fixed with the combat you learned on the Falklands. It is your duty to protect them from threats. Inside and out?"

"That's what I'm doing."

"Not when you neglect their needs. It's plain that I can help, but even more than me the Cape needs you. To be the guardian they can rely on. A leader that they can trust. To make the best decision even if it's unpopular. Are your principles really worth more than your lives? Would you die with pride rather than live with some compromise? Will you be small? Shrinking to the past. Drowning in quicksand of trespasses long ago? Or will you champion the future? Will you save them? Will you care? Will you rise? Am I worse than death? This might be your last chance."

Patricia paused in animation. Her gaze fell to the sand. Her muscles were still clenched, pulsing. Solus kept his distance. Looking away, her posture dropped. Her eyes drooped. She search the sand. Then cried. One tear after another until she collapsed into a trembling sob. The truth hurt so much she couldn't stand. *Why?*she asked.

"Before I give you my decision," she swallowed, "I have to know. When did Tiberius betray me? When did he tell you everything I told him?"

245

KING PENGUIN

Buckled in the sand, her strong voice transformed to a quiver.

Solus approached cautiously, etching from the dark. "When I started telling him everything you weren't. Truth floats. Even when you try to suppress it, eventually, it will find a way to the surface. Your omissions kept him dormant, but beneath he was thirsting for deliverance. I gave him this. Loyalty is always strongest for the liberator."

Patricia wept. Water ran down the side of her face curling down her neck. She had known Tiberius his whole life. Loved him like the fledgling she never could have. He listened when no one else could. Keeping her secrets like the truest friend. What did he want to say? What was it he couldn't he tell her? Was he afraid? Afraid of her? Grief, shock and hurt clenched in the pit of her stomach. It was compounded by a searing guilt. She wasn't there for him the way he was for her. She hadn't paid attention. Hadn't asked or listened.

Solus slid closer, talking softly, his shadow overlapping hers. "This is hard. It's a terrible feeling to be betrayed." Solus moved closer still. Patricia wept. "You've made some mistakes in the past. Yes, but I can fix them. I'm here to help. All you have to do is allow me."

His voice was now directly above her. She looked up blinking to clear the blur. "You are evil. Your father left you. Your mother hated you. I would have too if I was her. You're a worthless speck of scum. You deserve it. You deserve to have nothing. You

246

deserve to be nothing. You deserve to be alone. You deserved to be Banished. I won't give you our Cape to poison like you've done everything else. Nobody cares about you Solus. No one ever has. No one will."

Patricia stared blankly, and then dropped back into a gentle sob. Solus would never have the Cape, for exactly the same reasons he wanted it. She just needed to be sure on one thing. Solus took her only good friend.

Solus' glowing red eyes swelled as his body peaked in temperature. His chest pumped with hot air. He clenched his iron talons staring down at the top of her head. He moved to the left, posturing for the strike. One hard thrust would impale this sharp metal into her sad, sobbing body. He etched closer, his darkness slivering over her body more. He steadied his breath and lifted the metal to end her world. A slow blinking glint in the distance caught his sight. A better way. He lowered his claw, and left, and left Patricia still in her sorrow.

Chapter 50

Pierre feared the other side of this island. The vacant monuments from the Great Excavation loomed as a painful reminder of the decision he had not made. His mortal heart was swarmed and haunted by warm palpitations whenever he dared to recollect. He loved Emily. Their time together was real, but how do you choose?

Pierre traversed the frozen island toward Paul Jaunty's dome. His parents, ironically, had a similar start. With a set of decisions before them. Each spinning radically different outcomes. How did they choose? His dad didn't decide to flee with his aunt Patricia. He chose not to take that chance when he could've gotten out. But was his dad's life *better* for it? Why did he stay? Pierre wished he could talk to him now.

The troubled King walked the quiet white island wrestling with the stubborn conundrum. His aunt's words hung in his mind: 'Family first.' But in the gaps between other thoughts, he only thought of Emily. Was *she* his family now?

A clearing ahead revealed a small structure as a blip. What Pierre knew to be Paul's home manifested in the distance. This break along with Paul's humor and opinion was welcomed. He rushed up to the dome, slightly shrouded by grey fog, before he noticed an oxford trail inked into the ice. The somewhat faded trail smeared, messy and wide. It bent around the rubble. Pierre followed. His gaze crawled up the path to a mangled body.

"Paul?" He stepped lightly as if not to wake him up. "Paul?"

Pierre tapped Paul He didn't move. He pushed Paul. He rolled back limp. Pierre bent over the scarred body, sprinkling it with droplets.

"It's okay. It's okay." Pierre lay next to his friend. His cheeks trembled, hot breath launching tiny clouds of smoke. Pierre's chest sunk on that grim grey island. Though it was said adults were not supposed to cry, he did it anyway. *Who did this?* He said he had no friends. Who else could've known where he lived? Who else has even been here. Pierre turned his neck. Thinking. Delio? Who was he? That bird from the Great Excavation. Pierre rose, asking the questions he should have asked at the festival. Who was he? Where was he from? Which colony did he come with? Pierre examined the toppled structure. Then, his dead friend. He looked across the sea in the direction where his old home would be. Anger boiled within him. He then turned toward Caterwaul. *Delio Egnever. Delio Egnever. Delio Egnever.* He looked at Paul one long last time. Then lept *furiously* into the water.

Chapter 51

Booms from the drillship rattled through the ocean. Solus swam up alongside the corroded hull of the ship. The bulging steel moaned. The pressure inside must've been building ever since the Cape tried to remedy this little problem. This was Tiberius' greatest contribution. The plugs were successful at stopping the toxin from flowing into the water, but with nowhere else to go, the dangerous substance pushed against every centimeter of the swollen frame.

Solus admired the series of sculpted plugs. The ingenuity was a shining example of how well they could have served him. One peg of talc was pushed deep into each of the four different sized holes. Solus pressed the side of his face to the ship. Listening to it's moan like a womb. Then he raised his sharp reinforced talons, kicking the obstructions loose, one by one. The off-white rocks shot into the blue Atlantic and a flood of shiny, black, silky liquid rushed into the sea.

The stuff coming from inside the ships spread wide like tree roots instantly darkening the surroundings. The prophecy of death

Solus promised in his Banishment was now taking form. This was a victory. Not the one intended, but the one they deserved. The proper response to a lack of compromise. He only wanted to have the colony for himself. To lead. To rule. To return the favor of pain and agony yes, of course, but to also build his home anew. His clash with Patricia forced upon him an aggravating truth. There is simply no reasoning with idealists. He understood, now, how deeply burrowed the Cape's lack of love for him was. When offering himself as a savior even in their time of need, they would rather be wiped away than saved by *his* embrace. So be it. He would purge their broken system and cleanse their stubborn pride with the quotient of their disobedience. They didn't deserve the land they held. This deluge would wipe Caterwaul clean. So a new colony could start in its place. A proper society. A home made in his image. He would then be appreciated. He would be loved.

The thought of the Cape celebrating their fake independence, having wished farewell of their endeared King penguin, now playing in the ocean with their new families made Solus grin. The poison was coming. It was released. And it is on its way.

Chapter 52

"I thought you were gone," Aria squeaked in high-pitched voice.

Xander, Colt, and Puddles spun around.

"I was," Pierre said breathless from the fastest swim of his life. "But—"

"Tentacles! It's a giant octopus! It's the great squid!" Ethell yelled, hobbling hurriedly toward the group. "Tentacles! Shiny tentacles. In the water!"

Aria frowned. "That doesn't make sense."

"It does," Pierre said. "He released the poison."

"Who?" Colt asked.

The four looked down in shock at Colt's square face and boxy figure. This was the first time he ever spoke. His voice ribbited like a frog.

"Solus," Pierre responded.

Aria shook her head. "Solus is gone. Probably dead."

"He's not."

"How do you know?"

"I do."

"How!" she shouted.

The other members of the group bickered in debate.

"Because he told me. Right to my face what he was planning to do. And thought I'd never find out or at least not until it was too late. He introduced himself at the Great Excavation as Delio Egnever."

"So," Aria looked up. Then blinked. "Oh, no." The sudden revelation bleached her expression.

"He lured me away with a lie that it was safe. That my parents wanted me back. I didn't know who he was, but it didn't matter. I probably would've believed anyone."

"I'm sorry, Pierre." Aria's voice soft as petals.

The muscles in his jaw pressed his beak together. "The pollution in the water is from holes in the ocean skimmer."

"We plugged those," Xander said.

"They've been unplugged!" Pierre replied to Xander, standing over him.

"Right now, we have to get everyone out of the water."

"How are we going to get them to shore?" Puddles asked.

"The ones that are feeling well enough can latch on to our back and we'll swim them in. Just like Resistance Drills."

Colt departed quickly.

Pierre turned to Puddles. "Tell the Sachem. Rally every Catcher in the Academy that isn't out to sea. This is the most important haul of their lives."

Puddles nodded and disappeared.

Pierre shifted to Xander. "I need you to tell the albatross, Pickers, Couriers, and Messengers to fly over and scan. When they see stranded birds in the water, circle above so we'll know their location. We'll need those markers in the sky."

"Or the albatross could do the work for us and we can stay here," Xander responded.

"Shut up, now! This is no time to argue. Penguins are too heavy. We'd sink the albatross. It has to be us. Go!"

Xander trudged away.

Pierre clicked to Aria. "Okay we're the strongest swimmers. We need to be the first in the water. Avoid the contaminant at all costs. The darker the water the bigger the threat. The faster this happens the better. Remember, *Solus is here so be careful*."

As Pierre and Aria cut toward the sea, a tiny three-letter word drifted into Pierre's ear. *"Dad?"*

Chapter 53

Chills tingled over Pierre. Time stood still. He turned around. The little penguin stood so small that nearly a fourth of his body was buried in sand. His face was nearly all cheeks, and everything other feature seemed to work around them. His disproportionately big, round eyes shimmered with flecks of light brown and emerald. Pierre glanced to the fixture around his neck. Emily.

Aria crept next to Pierre, but stayed a half-step behind him. "Congratulations," she whispered weakly.

Pierre stepped forward. His shedding feathers wasn't his annual molt. It was the growing of his brood patch. That strip of bare skin which comes once a penguin is to be a parent. Pierre exhaled with marvel and wonder. The night atop the Toboggan Trails. If he had only known.

"Yes, it's me," Pierre said smiling. "Dad."

The little penguin put his chin in his chest and stirred the sand beneath him with one foot.

"Pierre!" Emily raced to his body, pressing her face against his.

"Pierre, I have to go," Aria quipped. "I mean, the team and I are going to help. We hope to see you out there." Aria paused. Then walked away.

"I was only a few steps behind," Emily explained frantically. "When he shot off running. He's so small. For a moment I lost track of him. What is happening here?" Emily peered across the Cape.

"Poison," Pierre said calmly, bending down. "In the water. And what's *your* name?" Pierre said to the tiny penguin.

"Timmy," replied a small voice.

Pierre smirked at Emily. Then looked back down to Timmy "That's *my* daddy's name. Are you *my* dad?"

The little penguin laughed.

Emily touched Timmy at his shoulders. "I figured this could give you a little piece of home."

Water seeped into Pierre's vision.

"What are you going to do about the poison?" she asked.

"Citizens in the sea. Catchers are the strongest swimmers. We have to save them," Pierre spoke slowly, as if in a trance, never looking up from Tim.

"*You're going in?*"

"Have to. They need our help."

"Umm!" Emily motioned from Timmy to herself.

"Can't think of only me."

"You can."

"I refuse," Pierre rose.

Emily stepped forward. "Listen. You are not going to leave me. I just watched my mom die. We came here to be a family. Start anew. Timmy & I can't have that, can't *be* that without you." The words spluttered out like hot water. Emily glanced at Tim, then whispered above his head. "This is *their* Cape, Pierre. *Theirs*. Not yours. You've done enough," she begged. "I need you. *We* need you."

Pierre gazed at his son, now tucked under Emily's wing. "Emily I'm sorry..." She shook her head and pulled away. "If I don't go to help a lot of other penguins will lose parents. If I could save them, you would want me to try, right?"

Emily looked him in the eye, "To be honest, I'm not sure."

Pierre sighed. "I love you." Pierre stooped once more, shifting focus to Timmy. "I'll make you a promise. I'm going to come back. I'm going to spend my life with you. And I'm going to be your father."

"Okay," Timmy said, partially burying his face into mother's side

Emily jittered. "I understand why, but I don't care. I just want to have something. Something actually good, without it being taken away."

"I'm coming back to you. I'm coming back for you. I won't leave you" Pierre whispered in her ear as she wept. He hugged

257

them in a long embrace nestling his head against hers first, then his son's.

In that instant, Patricia ran up. She glanced from Pierre to Emily to Timmy, appearing to put the pieces together. "Come with me," she said to Emily, "we can use your help with the ones that have brought to shore."

Patricia pressed Emily down the sand with Timmy at her side. Patricia looked back over her shoulder. She looked at Pierre with a concerned smile.

Chapter 54

"Pierre!" Aria yelled trudging out of the sea. She eased a massive black-footed penguin to the sand. "It's gotten thicker!" She shouted. Then splashed back in.

The small lot of penguins who made it back to shore on their own were gagging and wheezing. Being lapped by the flow of the surf. Catchers were already dropping off the first rescuees who were dripping with slime.

Pierre rushed to the break of the ocean when something dark caught his peripheral. He shot a quick glance to his left and recognized an unforgettable face. His expression was poised as he lingered just beyond the commotion in a vacant plot of sand. Pierre didn't think. He burst in his direction, slicing through the growing swarm of panic. The statue-like figure stared solely at Pierre as if they were the only ones there.

"Killer! Murderer!" Pierre growled.

"Thief," Solus returned. "You stole my Cape. But what's in a name?"

Pierre marched closer.

"Shut up! You're a liar!" Pierre shouted.

Solus laughed, "But, you were so easy. So eager to believe *anything* good."

Pierre felt like he was clenching every muscle in his body as he stomped.

"Oh! But, I can't take all the credit. I had help from your friend."

Tiberius tripped trying to duck into a dome and made a loud puff in the sand. Pierre's gaze burned through him with rage like fire. Tiberius kick-pushed himself into the dome until his body was covered by the shadow.

Pierre stared into the dark dome. Tiberius had betrayed everyone. He helped him do this. He *gave* Solus information about the oil. Pierre's parents. And who knows what else. Pierre took a slight step toward the dome before Paul's mangled body flashed in his mind. The frozen, twisted, open heap. His friend. Pierre clicked back to Solus, moving more quickly. Solus was grinning, thinly smiling, as if attempting to contain his joy.

"You *killed* my friend!" Pierre yelled.

Solus arched his eyebrows. Then shrugged.

"I won't let you kill anyone else." Pierre reached Solus and moved in close. The King penguin was only slightly taller than the Fiordland standing straight up.

KING PENGUIN

Solus lowered his beak passively. "But there's only one left,"
Solus grumbled, lifting the iron talons he had hidden under the
sand.

Chapter 55

Patricia and Emily raced along the shore with Timmy in tow. A field of oiled penguins lay moaning in the sand. They came to a dead stop as the few Medics well enough to work, switched between ailing patients. The Cape's primitive medicines seemed to do nothing against this heightened sickness. Seaweed wraps and aquatic plants didn't look to be helping, and frustrated Medics appeared to wear this reality openly. Their Medics spent their entire lives dedicated to wellness. The repair of the penguin body. Yet, in the moment the Cape needed their expertise the most, they were helpless as any other penguin.

A gurgling, wet cough popped nearby and made Emily shudder next to her. Patricia knew what it looked like. When there was likely nothing left to do but comfort. She pointed Emily to a nearby body then dropped to tend to the penguin in the sand at her feet. Emily lowered slowly and talked gently to the elderly Gentoo. The victim's feathers had begun to shed. Exposing stretches of bare skin on her face and neck. The old Gentoo seemed to search somewhere beyond Emily's face before her eyes finally refocused.

KING PENGUIN

Patricia glanced over at Emily, while stroking the head of a regurgitating Adelie.

Patricia could hear Emily talking to the victim.

"The world is better off for having you. You're loved. The ones you leave will keep you in warm memory." Emily smiled as Patricia witnessed the elderly Gentoo sink a bit more. Emily looked up at Patricia. Then over her shoulder. She frowned. She rested the elderly penguin's head in the sand.

"Have you seen Tim?"

Patricia peered past Emily to the small pit where he was standing, and shook her head. Emily looked back down at the Gentoo, who had now settled to sleep. Rising to for a full view, Emily cawed loudly and listened for a response. Patricia stood, calling for Timmy's father.

"I've got to find him," Emily said panting.

Patricia nodded firmly. "Let's go."

Sloshing down the shore, calling and spinning around looking for Timmy, Patricia held out a flipper and stopped Emily as something massive threatened to trample them both. Their beaks loosened, looking up as the giant sight stomped past them. Patricia peered up ahead. There were dozens of them. *Less-hairy Tree Dwellers*. Some were the color of day. Some were the color of night. Some were the shade of the sun and others the sand. Moving in giant leaps. Abducting citizens and planting them in strange floating objects. A fleet of the strange floating constructs eased onto the shore in the distance. The penguins well enough to move cowered and fled from the stomping titans. In that instant, two wide stretched arms reached for Patricia and Emily. They ducked and split around the figure.

"They're putting them in there! Check the floating things!" Patricia yelled.

The oblong, brown objects were rammed low into the sand. Emily and Patricia were barely able to hop up and peek inside the wooden transports. Hopping alongside Emily and stretching her neck, Patricia got flashes down inside of dozens of flustered, oil-drenched penguins.

Landing, a gravelly, dragging noise snatched their attention. One of the objects dislodged and floated limply into the ocean.

Patricia thought. *Did Timmy run off to find Pierre?*

Two more floating objects slunk off and pushed out into the Atlantic.

"We have to keep looking!" Emily shouted.

Scurrying from one construct to another, the mother was systemic. Hop. Peek. Call. Hop. Peek. Call. Patricia saw Emily straining to hop higher with each effort. They split up as the objects departed more rapidly. Dipping and slipping between the series of snatching hands which seemed to fall from the sky. Shortly, only three boats remained. Patricia checked to see if Emily had any luck. As Emily leapt high as the object ripped away from the shore. While Emily was in the air, the movement of the vessel knocked in the stomach and tipped her inside.

Patricia's face fell in horror. "Emily!" she screeched. "Emily!"

Chapter 56

Solus lunged at Pierre. His beak hissed by both sides of Pierre's throat. Pierre dodged the attacks thinly, bobbing left to right. Pellets of sand rained from Solus' metal contraption as he lifted and lunged it forward aiming at Pierre's gut. Pierre jumped back as the blades reached full extension then recoiled. Pierre staggered as his momentum carried him into a backpedal. Solus charged just before Pierre stuck a stance.

Pierre slipped to the side and landed a hard flipper on Solus' back. A gust of wind sprung from the Fiordland's body. Pierre followed with a blow to his head. Solus ducked under the limb before it connected. Stumbling forward, Solus head-butted Pierre in the stomach. Pierre hunched over and shuffled back. Solus stepped up and swung wildly. Pierre managed to bat down one attack after the other. Solus shuffled forward and plunged his trident of claws deep into Pierre's gut.

KING PENGUIN

Pierre released a blood-curdling screech. Solus pushed forward. Driving them deeper. Pierre let out a second horrific scream. Blood from the punctured flesh oozed around the sharp, metal talons. Pierre yelled, clapping his flippers hard on both sides of Solus' head. The Fiordland crumbled in a splash, yanking the claws from Pierre. Wincing, Pierre dragged forward unsteadily. Solus crawled away. Tried to stand. Stumbled. Tried to stand again, half-twirled and dizzily face-planted in the sand.

Pierre closed the space between them. Grimacing, Pierre stood at the base of his enemy. Solus flipped over fast and struck him with a kick. Something snapped. Pierre's left leg was in searing pain as Solus dragged himself like a turtle toward the sea. Pierre doubled over. He tried to step and the pain shot through his body once again. Pierre squinted, looking up. Solus had reached the edge of the surf. Hopping on the other leg Pierre gimped in pursuit. Solus was being swallowed and dragged in by the waves. Pierre tried to hop faster. Reaching the ocean he tripped and the hard slap of the salty water bit at his open wound. The tide pushed him back. Then pulled him in. Beneath the surface, the dark, stained water was a dim grey in the general infected area with random pockets of pitch black where the poison was more heavily concentrated.

Bubbling through a light grey haze, small fiery circles stared back at Pierre. Frowning from his injury, Pierre scrunched his neck and strained to pick up speed. He couldn't let him escape. Pierre had seen what Solus was. He had seen penguins like him back home. Saw what they grew to become. Solus was bringer of death. If left alive, someway, somewhere more were sure to die.

This would not become the Falklands. Pierre refused to watch his son grow up the same way he did. Pierre blazed further into the tainted sea. The once clear blue ocean was spotted like a leopard with poisonous black zones stretching three or four body lengths. Solus shot directly into the black haze. Pierre swam in after him. Then a second. And a third. And a fifth. Each time they rifled through the blinding poison, the light went out and Pierre was blinded. Yet each time he emerged, the gap had narrowed. Red flashes shot back sporadically through the aquatic. Pierre stroked harder. Feeling the harsh sting from his wounds. He kept his tattered leg close to his body so it wouldn't bounce with the flow of the water. Pierre pulled closer. And closer. He was so near now he could feel the drift coming from Solus' movement. Pierre stretched his neck to snatch Solus' foot before everything again went black. They disappeared into a pocket of liquid dark as starless space. Much larger than any they passed through before.

They were near the source. Pierre sensed Solus was close. Floating somewhere near. Pierre stopped and tried listened. Pierre knew just because he couldn't see him, didn't mean he disappeared. Solus hid here for the advantage. Releasing this poison from the ship, Solus effectively raised the deep sea to the surface. Creating a black pit. Similar to where Solus first gained the ability to *see* without light. An ability Solus was sure to be using right now. While Pierre was blind.

Pierre shook his head violently as the toxin seeped in through his shut beak. The taste of the oil on his tongue was sharp and bitter. Pierre blinked hard as it stung his eyes. Pierre floated in place. The substance burned as it reached into his open wounds. Pierre tried to focus and listen. He'd need oxygen soon. Pierre felt his thumping heartbeat. He opened and closed his eyes quickly. Solus' red light was nowhere to be seen. He opened and closed them quickly again. Darkness. Pierre rotated slowly. He opened his eyes and a flash of light split the dark. It was knifing toward him with blitzing speed. Pierre parried, creating a near miss.

He squinted, peering to the area where Solus bolted. The stinging substance once again forced them shut. Pierre hovered, blind and upright. *He needed oxygen.* But refused to let Solus get away. He closed his eyes tighter. He tried to listen more carefully. A tingling sound. It arced around him. It was very faint. Solus' iron claws clanged together as the water moved between them. Suddenly, the sound was moving in quickly. Pierre shot his eyes wide, ignoring the pain. Solus curved and swam across the width of Pierre's body, dragging the sharp metal across his chest. Pierre gurgled an underwater scream. A cluster of precious oxygen bubbles drifted to the surface. Pierre couldn't hold on any longer. He swam for air. He could see sunlight gently piercing the thick liquid near the surface. Pierre stuck his beak straight to the sky

269

sucking in the crisp air. He grimaced and let out another scream for the sting of the fresh cuts across his chest and the wounds in his belly. In that instant, Pierre saw a strange sight. A fleet of strange, floating objects, maybe twelve of them, were drifting away from Caterwaul. Pierre felt a stern yank at his foot and was snatched asunder.

Pierre managed to wiggle his foot loose. Solus quickly slithered up level with Pierre. Solus leaned and jousted his three sharp claws for Pierre's neck. Pierre swerved left and as Solus drifted past, bit hard on the high part of Solus' outstretched leg which carried the contraption. The Fiordland swam in a flurry, dragging Pierre as he clamped stubbornly to Solus' bone.

Solus beat down hard on the top of Pierre's head. One slap! Two slaps! Three slaps! Four! Pierre was jarred loose, along with the contraption as it was ripped free went sinking into the poisonous sea. Pierre's body s body awkwardly limp. The blunt force to his head knocked him into a fuzzy limbo. He heard voices as he floated, completely still. Flashes of rainbow colors pulsated and glowed in his mind's eye. Silhouettes, chatting in the mental fog.

"All I can say is family first."

"You've got a lot to live for now."

"*Something* good, without it being taken away"

"I promise."

"I need you."

KING PENGUIN

"Timmy."

"Paul Jaunty."

"I can see you still got the ooga baboogas!"

"Dad?"

The conversations marched closer. The sounds repeated themselves in succession. Louder. Closer. Louder. Closer. Louder and closer. Until they were jumbled in an incomprehensible mesh, screaming in his face. Pierre opened his eyes to Solus' red eyes just a breath away hovering in the pitch darkness, inspecting him. With lightning quickness, Pierre latched to his throat. Solus, twirled, swung, and slapped trying to pry Pierre off as he swam wildly like balloon losing air. The blows shot pain through Pierre's skull. Solus slapped his wounds. Pierre gritted and clamped harder. Patricia. Ferdinand. Solus pushed Pierre's face. Aria. Paul. Solus dug the tip of his beak into Pierre's shoulder. Pierre tensed. Emily. Timmy. Pierre squeezed so intensely his jaw clicked. Then, Pierre felt something like a shock go through Solus. Solus' struggle became less forceful. Solus' attacks now seemed like taps, asking for mercy. Pierre didn't give it. Pierre suffocated the monster until he could feel no more life, then held on longer.

Finally, Pierre released him into the ocean. The horrid red glow of Solus's eyes went dim, as the only light in the densely poisoned section of the sea, disappeared.

Chapter 57

After Emily vanished into the boat, Patricia was nabbed and plopped firmly into a different half-wooden shell. The penguins were inside the floating object were hysterical. A tall Galapagos struggled to hop over the ledge as a nearby group fought to keep her in. The party was being pushed to and fro by her raging, mad strength. Patricia watched as the penguin wailed and snapped. Hollering. Patricia witnessed the cause of her despair just beyond the edge of the contraption. Hordes of penguins bobbed in the ocean with the current. Motionless. Their floating object was drifting, parting the graveyard.

Patricia couldn't watch. As if not looking would change the reality. She wanted to protect the citizens. Wanted them to have peace, but in the end, she made this place just as bad if not worse than her own home. Patricia walked the length of the floating object. She winced from how roughly that hairless tree-dweller had snatched her from the shore.

KING PENGUIN

Patricia surveyed in the expressions of the shattered penguins. She knew she kept this secret from them. The poison. The timing of Solus' banishment, so she could make room for her nephew in the Cape. She let this happen. She made this happen. Set this in motion. She wasn't a protector. She failed her only purpose. Even Tiberius abandoned her. Where was her Ferdinand now? Her beloved mate? Was he floating amongst the corpses? Where was Pierre? Her brother's son she swore to protect? And his little son? Patricia sank. She thought she left death in the Falklands. But it found her again. Now, she learned it always would. It had taken everything with nothing left to start fresh. Patricia lifted her head to the sky as sunrays reflected in her watery eyes. She sighed. Tiberius. Ferdinand. Pierre. This was too much. She couldn't be strong. She couldn't bear. It was time to let go. Patricia hopped up on the ledge, wobbling as the contraction shook. She looked down into the shiny, dark , poisonous sea. Drew a full breath. And tipped herself in.

Chapter 58

The panic outside Tiberius' dome came to a steady hush. Tiberius hid, hoping to avoid the disaster on the Cape. Solus had stuffed him with delusions. Painting him as brave. Courageous. Doing what must be done. But, in this moment, he didn't feel brave. He didn't feel courageous. His alliance with Solus left him cowering in a dome, hoping never to see anyone who ever trusted him. Hoping never to see his own friends. That was what he now finally recognized them to be.

Tiberius peeked outside, ducked back in, then poked his head out once more. He squinted in the bright sunlight and his pupils constricted to a totally empty shore. His eyes sprung large. He stepped from the dome. He hobbled the length of the shore, with his bandaged wings. He yelled into empty domes. The Academy. Each time only hearing his own echo. He stopped on the shore, yelled once more, and collapsed. There were no Catchers bring him food. No Preservers to protect him from things of the forest. No Medics to help him heal. He lifted a bent wing and pain shot through half of his body. Tiberius hunched, whimpering as his wings hung heavy and crooked. He turned to the forest, then the ocean. Trapped between equally dangerous environments. Each with sharp-toothed predators preying on the sick and wounded as easy meals. Tiberius's body sank, feeling doomed. He would wilt in this beautiful prison until nothing would be left but loose skin, and brittle bone.

Chapter 59

Twelve floating objects lurched toward the falling sun. The only things moving atop the sea. Pierre, his head above water, looked over at the completely bare shores of Caterwaul. He paused. Then, turned and swam after the floating objects. The effects of the poison started to mount as his energy sank. He felt a sludge in his chest. A harsh dryness in his eyes. His lungs felt like they were partially filled with thick goo. The searing wounds across his chest and in his belly burned as he swam. He stroked desperately. Approaching the furthest behind in the fleet. Pierre pitifully arced alongside the object. Quick, blurry images of penguin huddled in crèches flashed as he caught a glimpse inside the carriers. Pierre flopped back into the ocean, pressing harder now. The penguins were in these objects. He hopped alongside two more vessels. The last of his depleted strength was drying up as Pierre was barely able to arc high enough to peek into the objects. He had taken on too much damage. His heart pumped in a thick, slow rhythm. Straining for more elevation, his body drifted to the side and locked mid-flight, crashing him into the sloped inner wall of a crowded transport.

Pierre shook. Convulsed. Oil dripped from the side of his face. Something blurry and large boomed toward him, pounding the wood beneath him, blocking the light. It opened his beak and pushed what felt like a small round eel deep down his throat. Pierre gaged. A cool liquid poured into his gut. Pierre started swinging with what life force remained, until his flippers were sternly pinned. A sharp stick was injected into his midsection then removed. The small round eel in his throat was reeled out of his body. Pierre gasped for air. The presence released his flippers and Pierre rolled to his side. Black gunk trickled from the corner of his beak into a slow-moving pool spreading away from him. His eyelids drooped to half-mass.

He was gently rolled over onto his back. A trembling Gentoo arrested him with a rough embrace as a small penguin rested his head on the place just below Pierre's chest wounds. Pierre sighed and dropped his head to the thick wood. He managed a smile with his eyes still half open. He had no clue where they were going. The Cape was no more. But, for now, they had each other and that was enough.

Epilogue

Navigating the field of bobbing corpses, one rescuer rounded back on grim hope of survivors. The ossified bodies of penguins bumped like thick logs against his hollow canoe. This was a vision unsettling to anyone who cared about the value of life. Not because it happened, penguins die every day like people do he thought, but because it didn't have to. As the field of penguins spotted the surface of this poisoned stretch of Atlantic, the only two sounds were the slow rolling whoosh of the evening waves and the gentle clang of his iron lantern as it hit the pole it hung from at front the boat. Time seemed to be in a sprint as darkness approached.

Standing up to peer far into the horizon one last time before turning in, the rescuer caught a glimpse of what he thought could've been a twitch in the far water. He steadied. Watched. He realized the shifting sea could create illusions of movement. Seconds passed. Maybe half a minute. *Something twitched again.* Mark pointed the nose of his canoe in that direction. Slowly, carefully sticking his oars through the gaps in bodies. When he arrived, he pulled the oars out of the water, reached down and plucked the bird from the thick slime. He laid the animal on his lap. The rescue worker split its beak pushing a medicated fish down into the bird's throat before its reflex kicked in to swallow the portion. *Good,* he thought. *Good.* The first signs of life.

The worker was thrilled. But many dangers still remained which could cause a swift death. He wasn't in the clear. Mark skipped down the ordered list of proper procedure, going straight for the mini-defibrillator he borrowed without permission. He was warned, using this at the wrong time could fry the penguin's heart. He clicked it on. He then charged the grips, rubbing them together. He took a deep breath and *shocked* the penguin once. The penguin's body resounded with a loud pop as its chest drew to the metal, arching its spine.

There was a climbing high-pitched noise, which peaked and faded. The instrument was ready to be used again. Mark delivered another charge. There was a deep choom as different muscles quivered and tightened everywhere across the bird. A rattle of the flipper. A shake of the foot. A roll of the torso. The bird stiffened, settling into a disturbing stillness.

The rescuer gritted his teeth looking away with the dead penguin stretched in his lap. Tears clouded his vision as streaks of beautiful purples, oranges, whites, blues, and golds raced across the South African sky. The rescuer sat in his canoe, in the newness of the quiet twilight, with the shock of what just happened. As the last bit of sun drained from his canoe, the lantern hanging from the pole at the front of his boat hummed to life. The lantern gently rapped against its pole in sync with the rhythmic waves. *Ting. Ting. Ting. Ting.*

Mustering courage to replace the cadaver back in the water for collections in the morning, Mark gazed down to a set of open eyes staring up, watching him. They were calm and quiet as if they'd been watching the whole time, with a breath so subtle it could barely be felt or heard. Mark brushed the drops of wetness which collected under his chin using the back of his wrist. He then cleared some hardened ooze from the bird's cheek. The rescuer smiled a wide, deep smile. The penguin shivered as the cold night air penetrated its now vulnerable coat of feathers since the toxic oil disrupted its natural ability to insulate. Mark fished something out of a small white plastic box, and carefully slipped a small emergency vest over the penguin's chest and flippers to avoid hypothermia.

Setting the bird down, Mark gently tiptoed over to the oars, setting course for the animal rescue center where the rest of the penguins were being held and treated. His sense of pride was enormous and brimming. He had dared to double back when others said there was no point and he saved a penguin hanging by a thread. In his crowning glory, he smirked, thinking how he must've saved the most unique penguin in the world. Eyebrows jagged as lightning. And eyes red as fire.

KING PENGUIN

This tale is in loving memory of:

Shirley Brown | Frank Byrd | John Ferguson

KING PENGUIN

Thanks For Swimming With These Penguins!